PENGUIN CLASSICS

A HERO OF OUR TIME

MIKHAIL YUR'EVICH LERMONTOV was born in 1814. After his
mother's death in 1817 he was brought up on his aristocratic grandmother's estate and separated from his father. Educated at home, he
made three journeys to the Caucasus and then studied in the Moscow
Noblemen's Pension and the University (1830–32), although without
sitting examinations. He then entered St Petersburg Guards' School
and began writing poetry and autobiographical dramas in prose. In
1834 he was made an officer in the Guards Hussars. On Pushkin's
death in 1837, Lermontov was arrested for a poem of invective
against Court Circles, *The Death of a Poet*, and was consequently
expelled from the Guards and sent to the army in the Caucasus. When
he returned to the capital he became involved in a duel and was
banished again to the Caucasus in 1840. He was twice cited for
bravery, but the Tsar refused to give him the award. On leave in
1841, hoping to retire and devote himself to literature, he was ordered
back to the forces. He was challenged to a duel by an officer, over
some trivial insult, and was killed on the spot. Lermontov is renowned as the one true Romantic poet produced by Russia and the
one who reflected most strongly the current trend of Byronism.
Many of his poems were set to music – *Borodino* and *The Cossack
Lullaby* became popular songs and *The Demon* was made into an opera
by A. Rubenstein. His other poems include *Mtsyri*, *The Prayer*,
Novgorod, *The Prophet* and *My Country*. Lermontov greatly influenced
Dostoyevsky and Blok; whilst Tolstoy and Chekhov regarded his
prose as a model.

PAUL FOOTE was born in Dorset in 1926. He is a University Lecturer
in Russian and Fellow of The Queen's College, Oxford. His publica-
tions include translations of Tolstoy's *Master and Man and Other Stories*
(Penguin Classic) and Saltykov-Shchedrin's *The History of a Town*.

M. Yu. LERMONTOV

A Hero of Our Time

Translated with an introduction by
PAUL FOOTE

PENGUIN BOOKS

PENGUIN BOOKS

Published by the Penguin Group
Penguin Books Ltd, 27 Wrights Lane, London W8 5TZ, England
Penguin Books USA Inc., 375 Hudson Street, New York, New York 10014, USA
Penguin Books Australia Ltd, Ringwood, Victoria, Australia
Penguin Books Canada Ltd, 2801 John Street, Markham, Ontario, Canada L3R 1B4
Penguin Books (NZ) Ltd, 182–190 Wairau Road, Auckland 10, New Zealand

Penguin Books Ltd, Registered Offices: Harmondsworth, Middlesex, England

This translation first published 1966
15 17 19 20 18 16 14

Copyright © Paul Foote, 1966
All rights reserved

Printed in England by Clays Ltd, St Ives plc
Set in Monotype Bembo

CONTENTS

INTRODUCTION

LERMONTOV is best known as the greatest Russian poet after Pushkin. *A Hero of our Time* is his only novel, yet it might be claimed that Lermontov owes his importance in the development of Russian literature almost as much to this one short novel as to his verse.

Lermontov's literary career spanned a mere dozen years before his early death in 1841, and *A Hero of our Time* was written towards the end of this time, in the years 1838–40. The period in which he wrote – the 1830s – was an important transitional stage in Russian literature, when verse surrendered its pre-eminence to the story and the novel, and the great age of Russian literature began. Lermontov's course ran parallel to that of Pushkin, his older contemporary, for both poets turned from verse to prose towards the end of their careers – Pushkin in works such as *The Queen of Spades* and *The Captain's Daughter*, Lermontov in *A Hero of our Time*, which was preceded by a number of other attempts at prose. Though Pushkin was unsurpassed by Lermontov as a poet, there is little doubt that Lermontov outstripped him as a prose-writer.

Lermontov is renowned as the one true romantic poet produced by Russia, and the one who reflected most strongly the then current trend of Byronism. He was certainly much influenced by Byron, but this does not mean that Byronic attitudes for Lermontov were something merely assumed. His life contained plenty of circumstances likely to produce a 'natural' Byronic figure. He was born in 1814, an only child, and lost his mother at the age of three. She had married somewhat beneath her, and after her death the boy was brought up by his indulgent and possessive maternal grandmother, seeing

7

little of his father, who was never on good terms with his mother-in-law. The divided loyalties of his family life and his comparative isolation in an elderly household helped to develop an introspective, brooding nature in the child. At fourteen he began writing verse, and his early lyrics are full of complaints of isolation, broken hopes and distrust of the world. Later his sense of alienation and bitterness were to be increased by unhappy love affairs. His childhood was spent mainly on the family estate of Tarkhany in the province of Penza, and the only notable events of this period were three journeys with his grandmother to the health resorts of the Caucasus. Here, though only a child, he was deeply affected, as so many Russian writers have been, by the magnificent mountain scenery and the exotic atmosphere of Asia. After four years of formal education in Moscow (including two fruitless years at the University), Lermontov entered the Cavalry Training School and two years later (in 1834) was commissioned in a Hussar regiment.

As a young officer in a fashionable regiment he moved in St Petersburg society, engaging in the usual pastimes of the capital and at the same time cultivating a cynical disdain for society, which he no doubt sincerely felt.

The four years before his death were the most eventful of Lermontov's life. In 1837 he sprang into the public eye on account of his poem *The Death of a Poet*. This was a savage denunciation of Russian society for the death of Pushkin, who had been killed in January 1837 in a duel which many felt had been deliberately engineered for the purpose of getting rid of the poet. The poem was regarded as inflammatory by the authorities and Lermontov was posted to a regiment in the Caucasus – in other words, sent into exile. He was now regarded as the poetic heir of Pushkin and the champion of his memory. Besides *The Death of a Poet* Lermontov wrote a number of other robust poems in which he showed that he was no languid romantic, but a poet of broad talents and a punishing social critic.

Though his exile lasted only a few months on this occasion, Lermontov was again despatched to the Caucasus in 1840, after being involved in a duel with the son of the French minister in St Petersburg. A year later, still in the Caucasus, Lermontov quarrelled with an acquaintance, a certain Major Martynov, over a trivial insult. They fought a duel near Pyatigorsk (the location oddly similar to that of Pechorin's duel with Grushnitsky in *A Hero of our Time*) and Lermontov was killed on the spot. He was twenty-six years old.

*

A Hero of our Time is what the title implies, an account of the life and character of a man who, Lermontov suggests, is typical of his age. The novel consists of five separate stories relating episodes in the life of this contemporary hero. Three of them were first published separately in the journal *Notes of the Fatherland* ('Bela' and 'The Fatalist' in 1839, 'Taman' in 1840), the other two ('Maxim Maximych' and 'Princess Mary') appeared only in the first full edition of the novel, which came out in May 1840. The novel continues the tradition of personal studies, initiated in Russia by Pushkin's *Eugene Onegin*, but with antecedents in western European literature, in which the contemporary young man with his problems and faults is exposed. That Lermontov was consciously creating a link with Pushkin's Onegin is shown by his choice of the name Pechorin for his hero. Pushkin had given his hero the name Onegin, derived from Onega, the north-Russian river; Lermontov echoed his choice by giving his hero a name derived from the even more northerly River Pechora.

Pechorin is, like Onegin, a representative of the so-called

'superfluous' men, who figure so often in the novels and stories of Turgenev, Goncharov, Herzen, etc. These 'superfluous' men were men set apart by their superior talents from the mediocre society in which they were born, but doomed to waste their lives, partly through lack of opportunity to fulfil themselves, though also, in most cases, because they themselves lacked any real sense of purpose or strength of will.

Unlike the classic type of 'superfluous' men, Pechorin is cast more in the mould of Byron's heroes, a strong individual at odds with the world. He is proud, energetic, strong-willed, ambitious, but, having found that life does not measure up to his expectations of it, he has grown embittered, cynical and bored. At the age of twenty-five (as he is in the book) he has experienced all that life has to offer and found nothing to give him more than passing satisfaction or interest. He sees that life has let him down, failed to provide for him the high purpose that would be worthy of his superior powers. So he is reduced to dissipating his very considerable energies in petty adventures of the type described in the novel. He embarks on these with few illusions that he is doing more than making a temporary escape from boredom.

The only comfort Pechorin has is his conviction of his own perfect knowledge and mastery of life. He despises emotions and prides himself on the supremacy of his intellect over his feelings. 'The turmoil of life has left me with a few ideas, but no feelings,' he tells his friend Dr Werner, and to prove it he rides roughshod over the feelings of other people. His disregard for the comfort and happiness of others is repeatedly demonstrated in the novel, and his victims are lucky if they get off with a broken heart (as Vera and Princess Mary) – the less fortunate (Bela, Grushnitsky) pay with their lives.

Pechorin is not just indifferent to the feelings of other people – he positively enjoys persecuting them, and though in some

cases the havoc he wreaks on people's lives is unplanned, in
others he sets out deliberately to destroy his victims. He talks
in his journal of his insatiable desire for power, of the pleasure
he derives from destroying others' hopes and illusions, and of
his view of other people as food to nourish his own ego. His
own frustrated ambition and resentment against life turn him
into a predator in the grand style. As he remarks during his
carefully planned campaign to win Princess Mary: 'There are
times when I can understand the Vampire.' It is particularly
this active, aggressive instinct that distinguishes Pechorin from
the common run of ineffectual heroes in Russian literature and
links him more with Byronic types such as the Giaour, the
Corsair, etc.

Pechorin's passion for contradicting others has been bred in
his own experience. His whole life, he says, has been a succes-
sion of attempts to go against heart or reason. Though in the
novel he claims that this conflict has been resolved in the victory
of reason over feeling, and prides himself on his immunity to
emotional experience, this is really a piece of self-deception.
He may be free from illusions about life, but he is still subject
to the power of his emotions. We see, for instance, the deep
effect that Bela's death has on him, the stirring of his old love
for Vera, his pity for Princess Mary even while he is destroying
her happiness. We see his vulnerability again in his moments of
self-pity, when he wonders why it is that people hate him (!),
when he himself feels dismayed at the destructive influence he
has on other people's lives and sees himself not as the controlling
genius of his actions, but as a mere instrument of fate. He even
has still some traces of the idealism which he possessed in his
youth. His sensitive appreciation of nature is partly due to his
recognition in it of the ideal purity and beauty which he finds
lacking in human society. He writes of Pyatigorsk in 'Princess
Mary': 'The air is pure, as the kiss of a child, the sun is bright,

the sky blue – what more does one want? What need have we here of passions, desires, regrets?'

It is in these moments of doubt and weakness that we see the tragic nature of Pechorin. Not only is he gifted with intellect and strength of will, he has also a poet's soul and a capacity for intense feeling. 'I've got an unfortunate character,' he tells Maxim Maximych in 'Bela'. 'If I cause unhappiness to others, I'm no less unhappy myself.' And we see that this is only too true. Pechorin is not just a dastardly villain of romance, but a complex figure, worthy of pity and understanding.

Talking to Princess Mary, Pechorin squarely places the blame for his character on the society in which he was brought up. He gives a pathetic account of himself as a child, full of noble ideals and impulses, but frustrated and mocked at every turn by the complacent mediocrities around him. The result, he says, was that he turned from goodness, truth, idealism to cynicism, hatred and evil. Though this confession is calculated to impress Princess Mary and win her sympathy, some part of it at least can be taken as the truth. Pechorin certainly is a social phenomenon. He belonged to the generation (Lermontov's own) that reached maturity in the decade following the abortive Decembrist Rising of 1825, which had resulted not in the hoped-for more liberal political régime, but in the stultifying repression of Nicholas I's reign. The generation which grew up at this time certainly had few opportunities for self-fulfilment, and Pechorin can well be seen as its product. Lermontov's title shows that he linked his hero specifically with the age in which he lived, and Belinsky, the contemporary Russian critic who was the first to give a detailed appreciation of the novel, emphasized that Pechorin-type figures were inevitable in that particular period of Russian history. 'This is how the hero of our time must be,' he wrote. 'He will be characterized either by decisive inaction, or else by futile activity.' It is obviously too much to follow the view of some Soviet critics who see Pechorin as a kind of revolutionary *manqué*, but it is reasonable enough to see him as an individualist in revolt against the mediocrity and conformism of his time, who, without an outlet for his talents, devotes himself to anti-social activities of the type described in the novel.

Pechorin is, though, more than a mere social type. He is also a psychological type, the dual character, in conflict with himself, torn between good and evil, between idealism and cynicism, between a full-blooded desire to live and a negation of all that life has to offer. This kind of character was one of Lermontov's continual preoccupations (well-known examples are the hero of his long poem *The Demon* and Arbenin, the wife-murderer of his drama *Masquerade*) and reflects, in part at least, the personality of the author himself. There is no doubt that Lermontov put a great deal of himself into the novel, and it was not surprising that on the novel's first appearance some critics claimed that in it he had merely portrayed himself and his acquaintances. It was this that led Lermontov to write the Preface (which appeared only in the second edition of the novel), in which he pours scorn on this idea, though, it may be worth noting, he does not reject it in so many words. Indeed, he could hardly have done so truthfully, for one or two of the characters were certainly based on real people, and in Pechorin's relationship with Vera there are echoes of Lermontov's own relationship with Varya Lopukhina. Though he might honestly say that he was not portraying himself in Pechorin – his presentation of the character makes that evident enough – there is no doubt, however, that Pechorin owes much to Lermontov's own experience. The disillusion, cynicism, frustration and hopeless striving recorded in Pechorin's journal are also found as recurring themes in Lermontov's lyrics.

Lermontov's attitude to his hero is critical, yet sympathetic.

He recognizes Pechorin's situation as a 'malady' (the diagnosis of which is the subject of the novel, though, as he remarks in the Preface, 'Heaven alone knows how to cure it!'), and he suggests that those who read Pechorin's journal will come to understand, and so excuse much that might otherwise seem reprehensible. 'Some readers might like to know my own opinion of Pechorin's character,' he writes in the Foreword to Pechorin's journal. 'My answer is given in the title of this book. "Malicious irony!" they'll retort. I don't know.' Of course, there is irony in the title, but it can be argued that the irony is aimed not so much at Pechorin as at 'our time'. Pechorin has 'heroic' qualities – energy, boldness, intelligence – but can do nothing with them, because he lacks any kind of purpose, and this is the fault of the time. Viewed in this way, the title can plausibly be taken as a vindication of Pechorin, fitted for a hero's role, but doomed to inactivity by his age.

*

A Hero of our Time is a landmark in Russian literature, for it was the first example of the psychological novel in Russia. A decade earlier Pushkin had written his 'novel in verse' *Eugene Onegin*, and Lermontov was certainly influenced by Pushkin's study. But he exploited the greater freedom of the prose medium to create in Pechorin a figure of far greater subtlety and complexity than Onegin. Lermontov showed considerable skill in the way he presented his hero. Each of the five stories is complete in itself, each reveals some new facts about Pechorin's character. Though there is no plot to link the stories together, there is a rough chronological framework, which can be deduced. In fact, the order of the stories in the book does not correspond to the order in which the events they describe occurred. The episodes described in Pechorin's journal ('Taman', 'Princess Mary', 'The Fatalist') come last in the book, but precede chronologically the events of 'Bela' and 'Maxim Maximych'. By presenting the stories in this order Lermontov introduces the reader by stages into the complexities of Pechorin's character. First, there is the tale of his abduction of a Circassian girl told by the simple, good-hearted old soldier Maxim Maximych. Then, in 'Maxim Maximych', the author gives his own more sophisticated view of the hero, whom he observes in a chance encounter. This leads on to the core of the novel, Pechorin's journal, in which Pechorin conducts a detailed analysis of himself.

Despite its loose construction, the novel succeeds entirely in its chief purpose of revealing the hero's character and situation. But Lermontov shows that he is capable of doing more than write about disenchanted young men, and demonstrates the range of his ability by some first-class story-telling and descriptive writing. In 'Taman' and 'The Fatalist' the character interest is completely overshadowed by the interest of the narrative, and it is the description of the journey along the Georgian military highway and the figure of Maxim Maximych, rather than Pechorin, that are the most memorable things in 'Bela'. The rich variety of secondary characters – Maxim Maximych, the *poseur* Grushnitsky, Princess Mary, Vera, the native girl Bela, Caucasian tribesmen, smugglers, well-observed minor figures such as Vera's husband and the dragoon captain – though serving primarily to show up the personality of the hero or to motivate his actions, also extend the interest of the novel and give it air and life.

With the possible exception of one or two digressions in Pechorin's journal, nothing in the novel is superfluous, and the whole is dominated by a sense of balance and economy. Lermontov's prose is tightly-sprung and remarkably controlled, especially when it is remembered that there was no established tradition of Russian prose-writing at the time. His dexterity as a writer is seen to equally good effect in all the various styles employed in the book – in the terse narrative of action, in the analytical passages of Pechorin's journal, in the impressive descriptions of nature, in the witty, aphoristic exchanges of the drawing-room, and in the homely conversation of the old soldier Maxim Maximych.

A Hero of our Time was highly regarded by later Russian novelists, and one can find in this short novel many of the qualities that characterize their own works. Lermontov's analytical method and the sensitivity he shows in his treatment of nature and people are paralleled by the psychological approach and broad feeling for life that one finds in Tolstoy. His concern for the problem of evil and the complexities of the human personality foreshadow Dostoevsky's studies in this field. And, as a stylist, Lermontov can be seen as a forerunner of Chekhov, who regarded 'Taman' as a model of the art of short-story writing.

As a late example of the 'personal' novels that were so popular in Europe during the romantic period, *A Hero of our Time* has often been linked with other novels of this type, such as Chateaubriand's *René* and Constant's *Adolphe*. The tradition is certainly a common one, though it is hard to see in Lermontov's novel any direct influence of these earlier models. In fact, a comparison of *A Hero of our Time* with such works shows how considerable Lermontov's achievement was, for he succeeded in making his hero a more or less entirely plausible figure, with dimensions of life and reality, and at the same time he went farther than the constricted intimate field of his predecessors to produce an extremely robust novel of action. Unlike many works of this period, *A Hero of our Time* asks few concessions from the modern reader. It can be read and enjoyed for its own sake.

*

INTRODUCTION

The setting of the novel is the Caucasus in the 1830s. The Caucasus at this time was a new area of the Russian Empire, and though Georgia – south of the main Caucasus range – had been annexed to Russia in 1801, the mountain tribes in the north were still not subdued, and in the period of the novel were mounting a vigorous resistance to Russian expansion under the leadership of the chief Shamil. The Russians had a series of frontier-posts and forts along the so-called 'Line', which extended the whole breadth of the Caucasus from the Black Sea to the Caspian, to protect the settled parts of the territory in the north against incursions from the hill tribes. The terms 'left flank' and 'right flank' which are used in 'Bela' and 'The Fatalist' refer to this east–west defence line. Georgia was linked with the northern Caucasus by the famous Georgian military highway, which ran from Tiflis over the main ridge of the Caucasus to Vladikavkaz (modern Ordzhonikidze). It is along this road that the narrator travels with Maxim Maximych in 'Bela'.

*

The present translation has been made from the edition of Eikhenbaum and Naidich, published by the Soviet Academy of Sciences in 1962, which repeats, with corrections, the second edition of 1841. I should like to express my thanks to Mr T. G. Griffith, Dr Ronald Hingley and Mr J. S. G. Simmons, who have kindly read the text of my translation in whole or in part and made many valuable suggestions; also to Miss Elisabeth M. Robson for her careful reading of the proofs.
April 1965   PAUL FOOTE

AUTHOR'S PREFACE

THE Preface is the first and also the last thing in a book. It either explains the book's purpose or else defends it against the attacks of critics. But the reader doesn't usually care in the least about a book's moral purpose or about journalists' attacks on it, so he doesn't bother to read the Preface. It is a pity, especially in our country, where the reading public is still so naïve and immature that it cannot understand a fable unless the moral is given at the end, fails to see jokes, has no sense of irony, and is simply badly educated. It still doesn't realize that open abuse is impossible in respectable society or in respectable books, and that modern culture has found a far keener weapon than abuse. Though practically invisible, it is none the less deadly, and under the cloak of flattery strikes surely and irresistibly. Our reading public is like some country bumpkin who hears a conversation between two diplomats from opposing courts and goes away convinced that each is betraying his government for the sake of an intimate mutual friendship.

The present book recently had the misfortune to be taken literally by some readers and even by some journals. Some were terribly offended that anyone as immoral as the Hero of our Time should be held up as an example, while others very subtly remarked that the author had portrayed himself and his acquaintances. Again that feeble old joke! Russia seems to be made in such a way that everything can change, except absurdities like this, and even the most fantastic fairy-tale can hardly escape being criticized for attempted libel.

The *Hero of our Time* is certainly a portrait, but not of a single person. It is a portrait of the vices of our whole generation in their ultimate development. You will say that no man can be so bad, and I will ask you why, after accepting all the villains of tragedy and romance, you refuse to believe in Pechorin. You have admired far more terrible and monstrous characters than he is, so why are you so merciless towards him, even as a fictitious character? Perhaps he comes too close to the bone?

You may say that morality will not benefit from this book. I'm sorry, but people have been fed on sweets too long and it has ruined their digestion. Bitter medicines and harsh truths are needed now, though please don't imagine that the present author was ever vain enough to dream of correcting human vices. Heaven preserve him from being so naïve! It simply amused him to draw a picture of contemporary man as he understands him and as he has, to his own and your misfortune, too often found him. Let it suffice that the malady has been diagnosed – heaven alone knows how to cure it!

I

BELA

I WAS travelling post from Tiflis. The only luggage I had on my cart was one small portmanteau half-filled with travel notes on Georgia. Luckily for you most of them have been lost, but luckily for me the portmanteau and the rest of my things have survived.

The sun was already beginning to hide behind the snowy mountain tops when I entered the valley of Koyshaur. Roaring songs at the top of his voice, the Ossete driver relentlessly urged on his horses so as to reach the top of Koyshaur by nightfall. What a glorious place that valley is! Inaccessible mountains on all sides, red-hued cliffs hung with green ivy and crowned with clumps of plane-trees, yellow precipices streaked with rivulets; high up above lies the golden fringe of the snow, while below the silver thread of the Aragva – linked with some nameless torrent that roars out of a black, mist-filled gorge – stretches glistening like a scaly snake.

We reached the foot of Koyshaur and halted by the inn. A score of Georgians and hillmen swarmed noisily round the place – a camel caravan had halted near by for the night. I had to hire some bullocks to pull my cart up this confounded mountain, since it was already autumn and there was ice on the roads, and the climb some two miles long.

There was nothing else for it, so I hired six bullocks and a few Ossetes. One of them heaved my portmanteau on to his shoulders and the others helped the bullocks along, doing little more than just shouting.

My own cart was followed by another pulled by two pairs of

bullocks as if it was the easiest thing in the world, although it was piled high with luggage. I found this very surprising. The owner of the cart walked behind it, smoking a little Kabarda pipe mounted with silver. He was wearing an officer's frock-coat without epaulettes and a shaggy Circassian fur cap. He looked about fifty. His dark complexion betrayed a long acquaintance with the Caucasian sun, and his prematurely grey whiskers accorded ill with his firm step and brisk appearance. I went up to him and bowed. He returned my bow in silence and puffed out an enormous cloud of smoke.

'We seem to be going the same way.'

He bowed again without speaking.

'You'll be going to Stavropol, I expect?'

'Yes, sir. . . . Carrying government property.'

'Can you kindly tell me how it is that four bullocks can pull your heavy cart with no trouble at all, while six can hardly move my empty one, even with these Ossetes to help?'

He smiled craftily and gave me a knowing look.

'You won't have been long in the Caucasus?'

'About a year,' I answered.

He smiled again.

'Why, what of it?' I asked.

'Oh, nothing. Fearful rogues, these Asiatics are. Do you really think they're doing any good with all that shouting? God alone knows what it's all about! But the oxen understand them. You hitch up twenty bullocks if you like, but they won't budge an inch when they shout at them in that language of theirs. Dreadful scoundrels they are! But what can you do to them? They like to fleece travellers. . . . They've had it too soft, the villains. And just you wait and see – they'll have a tip out of you too. But I know them, they'll not catch me.'

'Have you served here long?'

'Oh, yes, I was here in Yermolov's time,' he said with some

dignity. 'I was a second lieutenant when he came to the Frontier,' he added, 'and I was promoted twice under him for actions against the hillmen.'

'And now you're . . .?'

'Now I'm with the Third Frontier Battalion. And what about you, if I might ask?'

I told him.

Our conversation ended and we walked on side by side in silence. At the top of Koyshaur we found snow. The sun went down, and immediately night followed day, as is usual in the south, but in the reflected light of the snow it was easy for us to make out the road which still climbed uphill, though now less steeply.

I had my portmanteau put back into the cart and the bullocks replaced by the horses. For the last time I looked back down into the valley, but it was completely covered by a thick mist billowing out of the gorges. There was no sound from below. The Ossetes crowded round me clamouring for a tip, but so sternly did the captain shout at them that they scattered in a moment.

'Ah, these people!' he said. 'They don't know the Russian for "bread", but they've learnt to say "Give us the price of a drink, sir". Why, I'd rather have a Tatar – at least he doesn't drink.'

It was still almost a mile to the post-station. It was so still all round that you could trace a gnat's flight by the sound of its humming. On our left lay the black depths of the ravine. Beyond it and before us the deep blue peaks of the mountains, creased with folds and topped by layered snow, stood out against the pale horizon, in which the last glimmer of twilight lingered. Stars began to twinkle in the dark sky and it struck me as odd how much higher they seemed than back home in the north. Bare black rocks stuck out on both sides of the road. Here and there bushes peeped through the snow, but not a single dead leaf stirred, and amid this deathly sleep of nature it was cheering to hear the snorting of the tired post-horses and the intermittent jingling of the Russian harness-bells.

'It'll be a lovely day tomorrow,' I said.

The captain made no reply and pointed to a tall mountain which rose up directly before us.

'What's that?' I asked.

'Gud-Gora.'

'Oh yes, what about it?'

'Look at the way it's smoking.'

Gud-Gora was indeed smoking. Light wisps of cloud crept along its sides, and on its summit lay a cloud so black that it seemed a blot on the dark sky.

We could already make out the post-station and the roofs of the huts around it and could see welcoming lights twinkling ahead, when a damp cold wind got up and moaned in the ravine, and it started to drizzle. I had barely got my cape on before we were in the thick of a snow-storm. I glanced at the captain with a look of awe.

'We'll have to spend the night here,' he said with annoyance. 'You'd never get over the mountains in a blizzard like this.'

'Hi!' he called to the driver. 'Had any avalanches on the Krestovaya?'

'No, sir,' answered the Ossete driver. 'But much snow ready to fall.'

There was no guest room at the post-station, so we were put up in a smoky hut. I asked my companion to join me in a glass of tea, for I had my metal teapot with me – my one comfort during my Caucasian travels.

One side of the cottage was built against the cliff, and three wet, slippery steps led to the door. I groped my way in and collided with a cow (the cow-shed takes the place of the servants' hall in these parts). What with bleating sheep and a dog growling, I had no idea which way to go. Luckily I caught sight of a dim light glinting to one side which helped me to find another door-like opening. I was presented with a scene of some interest. The roomy hut, its roof supported on two smoke-blackened posts, was full of people. In the middle of the room burned a crackling fire, laid on the bare earth, and the smoke, driven back through the hole in the roof by the wind, hung so thickly over everything that I was some time getting my bearings. By the fire sat two old women with a host of children and a lean Georgian, all of them in rags. We had no choice but to settle ourselves down by the fire and light our pipes, and before long the teapot was singing merrily.

'They're a pathetic lot,' I said, pointing to our filthy hosts, who were watching us in a sort of dumb stupor.

'As stupid as they come!' he replied. 'Believe it or not, but they're absolutely useless. And you can never teach them anything either. Say what you like about our friends the Kabardians or the Chechens – robbers and vagabonds they may be, but they're plucky devils for all that. Why, this lot don't even bother about weapons. You'll never see one of them wearing a decent dagger. There's your Ossete for you!'

'Have you spent long in Chechnia?'

'I had about ten years there with my company in a fort near Kamenny Brod. Do you know it?'

'I've heard of it.'

'Ah, those cut-throats gave us a time of it! They're quieter now, thank heavens, but once if you went a hundred yards from the stockade there'd be some shaggy devil on the look out, and you'd only to blink an eyelid and before you knew where you were you had a lasso round your neck or a bullet in your head. Grand chaps!'

'You must have had lots of adventures?' I said, spurred by curiosity.

'Oh yes, of course. I've had some adventures . . .'

Whereupon he fell to tugging his left whisker, his head bowed in thought. I was most eager to get some kind of yarn out of him – a desire common to all those who keep travel notes. Meanwhile the tea was ready and I took two travelling glasses from my portmanteau, filled one and set it in front of him. He took a sip and said as if to himself: 'Oh yes, I've had some adventures!' This exclamation raised great hopes in me. I know that these old Caucasian veterans like to spin a yarn. They rarely get the chance, since they may often spend four or five years in some god-forsaken place with their company and all that time have no one to say 'Hullo' to them (for the sergeant always says 'Good day, sir'). And there would be no lack of things to talk about, with strange wild tribes all round them, constant danger and unusual things happening. One can only regret that so little of this is ever put down on paper.

'Have some rum in it?' I asked my companion. 'I've got some white rum from Tiflis. It's turned cold now.'

'Thanks all the same, I don't drink.'

'How is that?'

'I just don't. I took an oath. Once when I was a second lieutenant, you know how it is, we'd had rather a lot to drink, and that night there was an alarm. We went out on parade half-tipsy and didn't half catch it when Yermolov found out. He was furious. Very nearly had us court-martialled. That's the way of it – you might go a whole year sometimes without seeing a soul, and with vodka on top of that – you're done for.'

At this I almost gave up hope.

'Take these Circassians, for instance,' he went on. 'Once they get drunk on *buza* at a wedding or a funeral, it's sheer murder. I had a narrow escape myself on one occasion, and that was at a friendly chief's.'

'How did it happen?'

'You see,' he began, filling his pipe and taking a draw, 'you see, it was like this. At that time I was with my company in a fort over the Terek. It's getting on for five years ago now. One autumn, when the convoy arrived with the stores, an officer came with it, a young fellow of twenty-five or so. He came to me in full uniform and said he had orders to stay on at the fort. He looked so trim and clean with his uniform all nice and new, I guessed at once that he'd only just come to the Caucasus. "Been posted here from Russia, I expect?" I asked him. "Yes, sir," he said. I took his hand and said: "Glad to see you, very glad indeed. You'll find it a bit dull here, so let's not stand on ceremony. Just call me Maxim Maximych, if you don't mind. And there's no need for full uniform, is there? Just wear ordinary dress when you come to see me." He had his quarters allotted him and settled down in the fort.'

'And what was his name?' I asked.

'His name was ... Grigory Alexandrovich *Pechorin*. A grand fellow he was, take it from me, only a bit odd. For instance, he'd spend the whole day out hunting in rain or cold. Everyone else would be tired and frozen, but he'd think nothing of it. Yet another time he'd sit in his room and at the least puff of wind reckon he'd caught a chill, or a shutter might bang and he'd shiver and turn pale. Yet I've seen him go for a wild-boar single-handed. Sometimes you wouldn't get a word out of him for hours on end, but another time he would tell you stories that made you double up with laughter. . . . Yes, he was a funny chap in many ways. Must have been rich too – from the number of expensive things he had.'

'Did he stay long?' I asked.

'About a year, it was. But how well I remember that year! He led me a dance all right, though I don't hold it against him – after all, some people are fated to have unusual things happen to them.'

'Unusual?' I exclaimed with curiosity, giving him some more tea.

'Let me tell you. There was a friendly chief who lived three or four miles from our fort. He had a son, a lad of about fifteen, who used to ride over to see us. Every day he came for one thing or another. And it's true, we quite spoilt him, Pechorin and I. And what a daredevil he was – a great hand at shooting or picking up a hat from the ground at full gallop. There was only one thing wrong with him – he had a terrible weakness for money. Pechorin once offered him ten roubles for a joke to steal the best goat from his father's herd. And what do you think? The next night he brought him along by the horns. Sometimes we teased him, and then he'd see red and go for his dagger. "Azamat," I used to say to him, "you'll cop it one of these days. You'll come to a bad end."

'Once the old chief himself came over to invite us to a wedding. He was marrying his eldest daughter and he and I were *kunaks*, so you see I couldn't refuse, even though he was a Tatar. We set off and got to the village with all the dogs letting out a howl to greet us. The women hid when they saw us, and those whose faces we did get a look at weren't much to write home about. "I had a better opinion of Circassian women," Pechorin said to me.

'I smiled. "You wait," I said. I knew what I was talking about.

'The chief's hut was crowded. These Asiatics, you know, like to invite everybody to their weddings. We were welcomed with due ceremony and shown into the best room. I took care to see where they put our horses though, just in case of anything unforeseen.'

'What happens at their marriage celebrations?' I asked the captain.

'Oh, nothing special. First the mullah reads a piece out of the

Koran, then the young couple and their relations are given presents. They eat, they drink *buza*. Then there's the trick-riding. There's always some filthy tramp on a miserable broken-down hack ready to show off and make a fool of himself to amuse the company. Then when it gets dark they have what we'd call a ball in the best room with some poor old fellow strumming away on a three-stringed . . . I can't remember their name, anyway it's like our balalaika. The girls and young chaps form up in two lines facing each other and clap their hands and sing. Then one girl and a man come into the middle and sing bits of rhyme at each other, anything that comes into their head, and the others join in the chorus. Pechorin and I were sitting in the place of honour when the host's youngest daughter comes up to him, a girl of fifteen or sixteen, and sings him a – what shall I say? – a sort of compliment.'

'Do you remember what it was she sang?'

'Yes, it was something like this, I think: "Our young horsemen are graceful and their coats silver-laced, but the young Russian officer is more graceful than they and he wears braid of gold. He's like a poplar among them, though he'll not grow or blossom in our garden." Pechorin got up and bowed, touching his hand to his forehead and heart, and asked me to reply. I know their language well, so I translated for him.

'When she had gone I whispered to Pechorin: "Well, what do you think of her?"

'"Charming!" he said. "What's her name?"

'"Bela," I said.

'She certainly was good-looking – tall and slim, with black eyes like a mountain goat's that looked right inside you. Pechorin was completely absorbed, his eyes never left her. But somebody else besides Pechorin was taken with the pretty little princess. His blazing eyes stared at her from the corner of the room. Looking closer, I saw it was my old friend Kazbich. He was one of those tribesmen you can't be sure about – if they're for you or against you. He'd roused a lot of suspicion, but had never actually been caught at any mischief. He used to bring sheep into the fort and sell them cheap, only he'd never bargain. You had to pay his price, for no matter what you did, he'd never come down. They used to say that he liked a trip over the Kuban with the guerrillas, and he looked a proper brigand too – small, wiry, broad-shouldered. And devilish smart he was too, I'll say that for him. His *beshmet* was always tattered and patched, but his weapons were mounted with silver. And his horse was famous through all Kabarda – and right enough too, for you couldn't imagine a finer one. Other horsemen were all green with envy – with good reason – and people tried several times to steal him and failed. I can see that horse now – black as pitch, with legs like steel wires and eyes as fine as Bela's. He was strong too – galloped forty miles at a stretch! And so well trained he followed his master about like a dog and even knew his voice. He never tied him up. The very horse for a brigand he was!

'That evening Kazbich was looking grimmer than ever, and I saw he was wearing a mail shirt under his *beshmet*. "He's got a reason for putting that on," I thought. "Must be up to something."

'It was stuffy inside the hut so I went out for a breath of air. Night was falling on the mountains and a mist drifted through the valleys.

'I thought I'd look into the shed where our horses were to see if they had fodder. And anyway you can't be too careful – I had a fine horse too and more than one Kabardian had eyed her fondly and said *Yakshi tkhe, chek yakshi*.*

'As I was making my way along the fence I suddenly heard

* A good horse, very good.

voices. One I knew at once – that young scamp Azamat, our host's son. The other one said less and spoke more softly.

"'What are they talking about?" I wondered. "Not my horse, I hope." So I crouched by the fence and listened, trying to catch every word. I was intrigued, but missed some of it because of the singing and talking in the hut.

"'You've got a wonderful horse!" said Azamat. "Why, if I was master here and had three hundred mares I'd give half of them for your steed, Kazbich!'"

'So it's Kazbich! I thought, and remembered the mail shirt.

"'Yes," said Kazbich after a short pause. "Yes, you won't find a horse like that in all Kabarda. Once I was on a raid over the Terek with the guerrillas, stealing Russian horses. We ran into trouble and got split up. I had four Cossacks after me. I could hear them shouting, the infidel dogs. There was a thick wood ahead, so I lay flat on the saddle and gave myself into the hands of Allah. For the first time in my life I insulted my horse with a touch of the whip. He went like a bird between the branches. Sharp thorns tore my clothes, dead elm branches hit my face. My horse leaped over tree-stumps and charged through bushes. I should have left him as we came into the wood and taken cover among the trees on foot, but I couldn't bear to part with him – and the Prophet repaid me! A few bullets sang over my head and I heard the Cossacks running after me, on foot now. Suddenly before me there was a deep ravine. My horse thought for a moment and jumped. His hind legs came away from the far bank and he was left hanging by his front legs. I let go of the reins and went flying into the ravine. That saved my horse – he sprang clear. The Cossacks saw all this, but no one came to look for me. They must have thought I'd been killed. I heard them rush to catch my horse. It was agony. I crawled through some thick grass on the edge of the ravine and looked out. The wood ended there, and I saw a few Cossacks riding into the clearing. Then out of the wood comes my Karagyoz and gallops straight at them. They rushed after him shouting and chased him for ages. One Cossack in particular nearly had a lasso round his neck a couple of times – I trembled and looked down and started to pray. A few seconds later I looked up and saw my Karagyoz going like the wind before them, with his tail streaming, and the infidel dogs trailing one after the other over the steppe, their horses quite done in. By Allah, it's true, as true as I stand here! I sat tight in the ravine till late that night, and suddenly in the darkness – what do you think, Azamat? – I heard a horse running along the edge of the ravine. It was snorting, neighing, stamping its hoofs – I could tell from the sound that it was my Karagyoz. It was him, my old comrade! . . . and we've never been parted since."

'I could hear him patting his horse's smooth neck and calling him various pet names.

'"If I had a thousand mares," said Azamat, "I'd give the lot for your Karagyoz."

'"*Yok*. No, thank you," answered Kazbich indifferently.

'"Listen, Kazbich," said Azamat, trying to get round him. "You're a good man and a brave rider, but my father fears the Russians and won't let me go into the hills. You let me have your horse and I'll do anything you want – I'll steal you my father's best rifle or sabre, anything you like. He's got a real *gurda* sabre – you only have to touch the blade against your arm and it cuts into the flesh by itself – your mail shirt would be no use at all."

'Kazbich said nothing.

'"The first time I saw your horse," Azamat went on, "he was twisting and leaping under you, his nostrils flared, the flint sparks flying from his hoofs. It did something to me, I don't know what, and since then I've thought of nothing else. I despised my father's best horses – I was ashamed to be seen riding them. How miserable I was! I'd sit on the cliff for days thinking of nothing but that black horse of yours with his graceful step and sleek back, straight as an arrow. He would fix his fiery eyes on mine as if he wanted to tell me something. Kazbich, I'll die if you won't sell me him," said Azamat, his voice trembling.

'I heard him burst into tears – and Azamat was an extremely stubborn lad, I might say, and nothing ever made him cry, even when he was younger.

'Kazbich answered these tears with what sounded like a laugh.

'"Listen. I'll do anything," said Azamat, his voice firm again. "What if I steal my sister for you? Think of the way she dances and sings! And the marvellous gold embroidery she does! Why, the Sultan himself never had such a wife. What do you say? Wait for me tomorrow night by the stream in the gorge. I'll take her along there towards the next village – and she's yours! Isn't Bela worth your horse?"

'For a long time Kazbich said nothing. Then, instead of answering, he softly sang the old song:*

> Our country has many a maid that is fair,
> With eyes starry black like the midnight air.
> Happy the lad who gains love's ecstasy,
> But happier the lad whose fancy is free.
> Wives can be bought for a pot-full of gold,
> But a mettlesome steed is worth riches untold.
> He races the wind on the measureless plain,
> For ever faithful and true he'll remain.

'Azamat tried hard to persuade him, but it was no use. He wept, flattered, swore promises, till at last Kazbich lost patience and cut him short.

* I beg the reader to excuse me for having put Kazbich's song into verse. It was of course given to me in prose, but habit is second nature. (M.Yu.L.)

'"Off with you, you silly boy! How could you ride my horse? Before you'd gone a couple of yards he'd throw you and you'd crack your skull on a rock."

'"Never!" cried Azamat in fury, and I heard the boy's dagger ring against Kazbich's mail shirt. A strong arm shoved him off and he hit the fence so hard that it shook. "Now for some fun!" I thought and dashed into the stable, harnessed our horses and took them out into the back yard.

'A couple of minutes later all hell was let loose in the hut. What happened was this – Azamat went running into the hut with his *beshmet* torn and said Kazbich had tried to kill him. Everyone leapt up, grabbed their guns – and then the fun began! Shouting, yelling, guns firing. But Kazbich was already in the saddle, weaving his way along the street like a demon and beating off the crowd with his sabre.

'I caught Pechorin's arm. "No point in getting mixed up in other people's quarrels," I said. "Let's get out of here quick."

'"No, let's wait and see what happens."

'"Nothing good, you can be sure of that. These Asiatics are all the same – they get their fill of *buza*, then out come the knives!"

'We mounted and galloped home.'

'But what about Kazbich?' I asked the captain impatiently.

'His sort never come to any harm,' he replied, finishing his glass of tea. 'He got away of course.'

'Not even wounded?' I asked.

'God alone knows. Brigands like him take some killing. I've seen them in action – stuck full of bayonet holes like a sieve, but sabre still swinging.'

The captain paused for a moment, then stamped his foot and went on.

'One thing I'll never forgive myself, though. When we got back to the fort I was fool enough to tell Pechorin what I'd heard behind the fence. He laughed, the cunning beggar. He was up to something himself.'

'What was it? Do tell me.'

'Oh, all right. Now I've started, I'd better go on.

'Three or four days after this Azamat came to the fort. He went in to see Pechorin as usual, for Pechorin always used to give him nice bits to eat. I was there. They started talking about horses and Pechorin sang the praises of Kazbich's horse. It was a beauty, he said, and nimble as a mountain goat – in fact, the way he went on you'd have thought there was no other horse in the world like it.

'The boy's eyes glittered, but Pechorin seemed not to notice. And if I started talking about anything else he'd at once get the conversation back to Kazbich's horse. Whenever Azamat came the same thing happened. In two or three weeks I noticed the boy was looking pale, like someone pining away from love in a story-book. I couldn't understand it.

'Well, I did get to the bottom of it later – Pechorin had so teased the boy he was fit to drown himself. He said to him once: "I see that you're crazy about that horse, Azamat, but you've no more hope of getting him than you have of flying. Tell me what you'd give to anyone who got him for you."

'"Anything he liked," answered Azamat.

'"Then I'll get him for you, only on condition. Swear you'll do what I ask . . ."

'"I swear it. . . . But you swear too."

'"All right, I swear you shall have the horse. But I want your sister Bela in return. Karagyoz will do as bride-money for her. I hope the deal suits you."

'Azamat said nothing.

'"You don't want to? Have it your own way then. I thought you were a man, but you're still a child, too young to be riding horses . . ."

'Azamat flared up. "What about my father?" he said.

'"Don't tell me he never goes away."

'"Yes, he does . . ."

'"Do you agree then?"

'"All right," whispered Azamat, pale as death. "But when?"

'"The next time Kazbich comes. He's promised to bring in a dozen rams. Leave the rest to me. And mind you do your part of the bargain, Azamat."

'So they fixed it up between them. A bad business it was too.

'I told Pechorin so afterwards, but he only answered that an uncivilized Circassian girl should be glad to have a nice husband like him, since, after all, according to their ways he would be her husband. And Kazbich, he said, was a brigand and deserved to be punished. I ask you, what could I say to that? . . . But at the time I didn't know about their plot. So one day Kazbich came in and asked if we wanted any rams or honey and I told him to bring some along next day. "Azamat," says Pechorin, "I'll have my hands on Karagyoz tomorrow. If Bela isn't here tonight you'll never see the horse . . ."

'"All right," said Azamat and galloped off to the village.

'That evening Pechorin armed himself and left the fort. How they fixed things I don't know, but during the night they both came back and the sentry noticed that Azamat had a woman lying across his saddle with her hands and feet tied and her head covered with a *yashmak*.'

'And the horse?' I asked the captain.

'I'm just coming to that. Early next morning Kazbich turned up with a dozen rams to sell. He hitched his horse to the fence and came in to see me. I gave him some tea – for brigand though he was, we were still *kunaks*.

'We chatted about this and that and then I suddenly saw him shudder and a look of horror come over his face. He rushed to the window, but it so happened it faced on to the back yard.

36

'"What's up?" I asked.

'"My horse, my horse!" he said, shaking all over.

'And in fact I did hear the clatter of hoofs.

'"It'll be some Cossack coming in . . ." I said.

'"No! *Urus yaman!*" he cries, "a bad Russian!" and rushes out of the house like a wild panther. In two strides he was outside. The sentry at the fort gate tried to bar his way with his gun, but he leaped over it and tore off down the road. In the distance there was a cloud of dust – Azamat galloping away on the fiery Karagyoz. Kazbich snatched his rifle from its case as he ran and fired. He stood still for a moment or two till he was sure he'd missed, then let out a wail and dashed his rifle against a stone so it broke in pieces. Then he fell to the ground and sobbed like a child. People from the fort gathered round him, but he didn't notice them. They stood and talked for a bit and then went back. I had the money for the rams put down beside him, but he didn't touch it, only lay there flat on his face as if he was dead. And believe it or not, he lay there like that the whole night through. Only next morning did he come into the fort and ask for the name of the thief. The sentry had seen Azamat untie the horse and gallop away and saw no need to keep quiet about it. At the mention of Azamat, Kazbich's eyes gleamed and he set off for the village where the boy's father lived.'

'What did the father do?'

'That was the point. He wasn't there when Kazbich turned up. He'd gone off for a few days, otherwise Azamat could never have carried off his sister.

'When the father got back he found both daughter and son gone. The boy was no fool, you see, and reckoned he'd be as good as dead if ever he was caught. He's never been heard of since. He probably joined some guerrilla band and got himself killed over the Terek or the Kuban. And jolly good riddance!

'This affair caused me some trouble too, I can tell you. As soon as I found out that the girl was in Pechorin's quarters, I put on my epaulettes and sword and went to see him.

'He was in the front room, lying on his bed with one hand under his head and the other holding a pipe that had gone out. The door of the inner room was locked and the key wasn't in the lock. I took all this in at a glance. I coughed and scuffed my heels in the doorway, but he pretended not to hear.

'"Ensign Pechorin!" I said as sternly as I could. "Can't you see I'm here?"

'"Ah, hullo, Maxim Maximych. Have a pipe, won't you?" he answered, without getting up.

'"Pardon me, I am not Maxim Maximych, I'm 'sir' to you."

'"All the same, won't you have some tea? You've no idea how worried I am."

'"I know all about it," I replied, going up to his bed.

'"So much the better. I don't feel much like telling you."

'"Ensign Pechorin, you have committed an act for which I too may be held responsible."

'"Oh, come now, why all the fuss? It's always been share and share alike with us, hasn't it?"

'"What do you mean by joking, sir! Your sword, if you please!"

'"Mitka, bring my sword!"

'Mitka brought the sword. Now that I'd done my duty I sat down by him on the bed and said: "Now look here, Pechorin, this won't do, you know."

'"What won't do?"

'"Why, your taking away Bela, of course. . . . That rogue Azamat! Come on now, admit it," I said to him.

'"What if I like her?"

'Well, what could I say? I was at a loss. Still, after a few

38

moments' silence I told him that if her father asked for her he'd have to give her back.

'"Nothing of the sort."

'"But what happens when he finds out she's here?"

'"How will he find out?"

'I was stumped again.

'"Look here, Maxim Maximych," said Pechorin, sitting up. "You're a kindly man. If we give that old savage back his daughter he'll slit her throat or sell her. What's done is done. There's no point in messing things up just for the fun of it. Let me keep the girl, and you're welcome to my sword . . ."

'"Show me her then," I said.

'"She's through that door, but even I couldn't see her today when I tried – she's sitting there in the corner wrapped up in her shawl and won't speak or look at you. She's as timid as a mountain goat. I've taken on the woman from the tavern – she knows Tatar and will look after her and bring her round to the idea that she belongs to me. For she'll belong to no one else!" he added, banging his fist on the table.

'I agreed again. What else could I do? There are some people you just have to agree with.'

'And what happened?' I asked Maxim Maximych. 'Did he manage to bring her round? Or did captivity make her pine away with homesickness?'

'Why should she be homesick? She saw the same mountains from the fort as she did from her village – and that's all these savages want. Besides, every day Pechorin gave her a present of some kind. The first few days she didn't say anything and spurned his gifts, which went to the tavern-keeper's wife, who waxed quite eloquent about them. Ha, presents! What a woman won't do for a scrap of coloured rag! But that's another story. Pechorin had a long struggle with her. Meanwhile he learned to speak Tatar and she came to understand something of our language. She gradually came round to looking at him, secretly at first out of the corner of her eye. She was still sad though and sang songs to herself in a soft voice that made even me feel sad as I listened in the next room. I'll never forget one scene – I was walking by and happened to glance through the window. Bela was sitting on the bench by the stove, her head bowed down on her chest. Pechorin was standing in front of her.

'"Listen, my fairy," he said. "You know very well you'll be mine sooner or later, so why torment me? You're not in love with some Chechen, are you? If so, you can go home at once." She gave a faint start and shook her head. "Or do you hate me altogether?" he went on. She sighed. "Or does your religion stop you loving me?" She turned pale and said nothing. "Believe me," he said, "Allah is the same for all races and if he allows me to love you why should he stop you loving me in return?" She gazed at his face as if struck by this new thought. You could see in her eyes that she was uncertain, yet wanted to believe. What eyes they were! They shone like two coals.

'"Listen, dear, sweet Bela," Pechorin went on. "You see how much I love you. I'd give anything to cheer you up. I want you to be happy, and if you're going to go on being sad then I shall die. Say that you will be more cheerful."

'She thought for a moment, her black eyes still fixed on him, then smiled sweetly and nodded her head. He took her hand and tried to get her to kiss him. She resisted feebly, just kept saying "Please, please, no, no." He became more insistent, she trembled and burst into tears. "I'm your prisoner," she said, "your slave. Of course you can make me do what you want." Then more tears.

'Pechorin struck his fist against his forehead and rushed into the next room. I went in to see him. He was walking up and down grimly, his arms folded. "What's up, old chap?" I asked him. "That's no woman, it's the devil himself," he said. "But I give you my word that she'll be mine . . ." I shook my head. "Do you want to bet?" he said. "I say she'll be mine in a week!" "By all means!" I said. We shook hands on it and parted.

'The very next day he sent a messenger off to Kizlyar to buy various things. He came back with a vast assortment of Persian cloths, I couldn't tell you how many.

'"What do you think, Maxim Maximych," he said to me as he showed me the presents. "Will the Asian beauty hold out against a battery like this?" "You don't know Circassian women," I said. "They're nothing like Georgian women or the Transcaucasian Tatars, nothing like that at all. They have their standards. They're brought up differently." Pechorin smiled and began whistling a march.

'As it turned out I was right. The presents did only half the trick. She grew more friendly, more trusting, but that was all. So he decided on the last resort.

'One morning he had his horse saddled, put on Circassian dress, took his weapons and went in to her. "Bela," he said, "you know how much I love you. I decided to carry you off thinking you would come to love me when you knew me. I was wrong. Good-bye. All I have is yours to keep. Go back to your father if you want – you're free. I've done you wrong and must punish myself. Good-bye. I'm going away. Where I'll go I don't know. I don't suppose it will be long before I can find death from a bullet or sabre-stroke. Remember me then and forgive me."

'He turned away and offered his hand in parting. She didn't take it or say anything. But from where I was behind the door I could see her face through the crack. I pitied her to see how deathly pale that sweet little face had gone. Hearing no answer, Pechorin took a few steps towards the door. He was trembling, and I might say I think he was fit to do what he'd threatened as a joke. That's the sort of man he was, there was no knowing him. But he'd hardly touched the door when she sprang up sobbing and threw her arms around his neck. Believe it or not, but I wept myself as I stood there behind the door. Well, not exactly wept, you know – oh, just an old man's silliness!'

The captain was silent.

'Yes,' he said, tugging at his whiskers, 'I confess I was upset that no woman had ever loved me like that.'

'Did their happiness last long?' I asked.

'Yes, she admitted to us that after she first saw Pechorin she had often dreamt of him and that no man had ever made her feel that way before. Yes, they were happy.'

'How dull!' I found myself exclaiming.

There was I expecting some tragic end only to have my hopes dashed in this unexpected fashion!

'Do you mean to say her father had no idea you'd got her in the fort?' I asked.

'Well, actually I think he did suspect it, but a few days later we heard the old man had been killed. It was like this . . .'

I was once more all attention.

'Kazbich, you see, had got the idea that the old man had connived at Azamat's stealing his horse. That's what I reckon, anyway. So one night he lay in wait for him on the road a mile or two from the village. The old man had been out trying to find his daughter and was on his way home. It was just getting dark. He'd got ahead of his men and was walking his horse, thinking things over. All of a sudden Kazbich springs out like a cat from behind a bush, jumps up on the horse behind him and fells him with his dagger. Then he grabs the reins and is gone. Some of the men saw all this from a hill. They dashed after him but couldn't catch him.'

'So he got his revenge and made up for the loss of his horse,' I said, hoping to elicit my companion's opinion.

'Of course, to their way of thinking he was quite right,' said the captain.

I couldn't help being struck by this capacity of Russians to adapt themselves to the ways of peoples they happen to live among. I don't know if this is a praiseworthy quality or not, but it does show wonderful flexibility and that clear common sense that can forgive evil wherever it is seen to be inevitable or ineradicable.

Meanwhile, we had finished our tea. The horses had long been harnessed and were shivering in the snow. In the west a pale moon was about to sink into the black clouds that hung like tattered shreds of curtain on the distant peaks. We left the hut. The weather had cleared, in spite of what my companion had said, and a fine morning promised. Far away on the horizon groups of dancing stars wove wondrous patterns, fading one by one as the pale light of dawn spread over the deep violet sky and lit up the virgin snow on the steep mountain slopes. Dark mysterious chasms yawned on either side of us. Wreaths of mist coiled and twisted like snakes, sliding down the folds of neighbouring cliffs into the abyss, as though they sensed and feared the approach of day. There was peace in heaven and on earth. It was like the heart of a man at morning prayer. Only occasionally a puff of cool easterly breeze ruffled the horses' frosty manes.

We set off. Five lean nags toiled up the winding road towards Gud-Gora with our carts, while we followed on foot, wedging stones under the wheels when the horses were winded. The road seemed to lead right up to the sky, for it went on rising as far as the eye could see, to vanish in the cloud that had rested on Gud-Gora since the day before, like a kite awaiting its prey. Snow crunched beneath our feet. The air was getting so thin that it hurt to breathe. The blood kept rushing to one's head. Yet for all that every fibre of my body tingled with ecstasy. I felt somehow happy to be so high above the world – a childish feeling, I grant, but we can't help becoming children as we leave social conventions behind and come nearer to nature. All life's experience is shed from us and the soul becomes anew what it once was and will surely be again.

Anyone who has chanced like me to roam through desolate mountains and studied at length their fantastic shapes and drunk the invigorating air of their valleys can understand why I wish to describe and depict these magic scenes for others.

At long last we reached the top of Gud-Gora. We stopped and looked round. A grey cloud hung over the mountain. Its chilly breath threatened an imminent storm, but the sky was so clear and golden to the east that the captain and I never gave it a thought. No, not even the captain, for a simple man feels nature's beauty and grandeur a hundred times more powerfully and keenly than rapturous story-tellers like me who write and talk about these things.

'You're used to this splendid scenery, I suppose,' I said.

'Oh, yes. Of course, you can even get used to bullets whistling past you – or at least to pretending not to feel keyed up.'

'I've heard, though, that many old soldiers find it music in their ears.'

'Well, yes, all right, you can even enjoy it. But only because it's so exciting. Look,' he said, pointing towards the east. 'What a marvellous place this is!'

And sure enough, I'm hardly likely to see such a view again. Below us lay the Koyshaur Valley with the Aragva and some lesser river crossing it like two silver threads. Bluish mist drifted down the valley, sheltering in the neighbouring gorges from the warmth of the morning sun. To right and left stretched intersecting chains of snowy, scrub-covered mountains, towering one above the other. There were still more mountains in the distance, though never two cliffs alike. And everywhere the snow shone with a ruddy glow, looking so bright and gay that one felt like staying and living there for ever. The sun peeped over the top of a deep blue mountain that only a practised eye could tell from a thunder cloud. A bloody streak lay over the sun and my companion eyed it with special interest.

'I told you we were in for a storm today,' he declared. 'We'd better hurry up or we'll get caught on the Krestovaya. Get moving!' he shouted to the drivers.

We put chains on the wheels to act as a brake in case they ran away, took the horses by the bridle and began the descent. On the right was sheer cliff and on the left a chasm so deep that an Ossete village at the bottom looked no bigger than a swallow's nest. I shuddered when I thought of the couriers who pass this way a dozen times a year. The road at this point is too narrow for two carts to pass, yet they go down it at dead of night and never even bother to get out of their jolting carriages.

One of our drivers was a Russian peasant from Yaroslavl, the other an Ossete. The Ossete unharnessed the leading pair and led the shaft horse by the bridle, going very warily. Yet all this time our good Russian blithely kept his seat on the box! I pointed out to him that he might at least spare a thought for my portmanteau, as I wasn't all that keen on scrambling after it into the ravine.

'Never you worry, sir,' he said. 'With God's grace we'll get there just the same as them. After all, we've done it before.'

And he was right. True, we might never have arrived, but the fact is we did. If only people thought a little more about it, they would see that life is not worth worrying about so much.

But perhaps you want to know how the story of Bela ended? First, though, I must remind you that I am writing travel notes, not a story, and so I cannot make the captain tell his tale before he in fact did so. You must therefore wait or, if you prefer, turn on a few pages – though I would advise you not to do this, for the crossing of the Krestovaya (or Mont Saint-Christophe, as the learned Gamba calls it) is well worth your attention.

We descended then from Gud-Gora into Chertova Valley. A romantic name! You picture to yourself the lair of the Evil One set among inaccessible crags. But you are wrong – the name Chertova does not come from *chert* 'devil', but from *cherta* 'boundary', for this was once the Georgian frontier. The valley was blocked with snowdrifts that brought back vivid memories of Saratov, Tambov and other such 'agreeable' parts of our native land.

We completed our descent.

'There's the Krestovaya,' said the captain, pointing to a snow-covered hill with a black cross on its summit. By the cross one could just make out the road, which is only used when the road skirting the hill is blocked with snow. Our drivers said there had not been any avalanches yet, so they took us by the side road to spare the horses.

At a turning we met half a dozen Ossetes who offered us their services. They seized the wheels and with much shouting set to pulling and steadying our carts. The road was certainly dangerous. On our right were piles of overhanging snow, looking as though the first gust of wind would send them plunging into the ravine. The narrow road was partly covered with snow. In some places it gave way under our feet, but in others it had been turned into ice by the sun and the night frost. We found the going difficult enough ourselves, and our horses kept stumbling. On our left yawned a deep chasm down which a torrent flowed, one moment vanishing beneath the crust of ice, the next leaping and foaming over black rocks.

We just managed to get round the Krestovaya in two hours. Two hours to cover a mile and a half! Meanwhile the clouds came down and it began hailing and snowing hard. The wind tore through the ravines, roaring and whistling like the Robber Solovey in the folk-tale. The stone cross was soon lost in the banks of mist that rolled in ever thicker and faster from the east.

There is, by the way, a strange, though widespread legend about this cross. It is said to have been put up by Peter the First as he was crossing the Caucasus. But, in the first place, Peter only went to Daghestan; and in the second place, it says on the cross in large letters that it was erected by order of General Yermolov, in 1824 to be exact. But in spite of this inscription, the legend is so well established that you do not know what to believe, especially as we are not used to believing what we read on inscriptions anyway.

We had to go down another three and a half miles over ice-covered cliffs and soft snow to reach the station at Kobi. The horses were dead beat and we were absolutely frozen. The blizzard howled more and more furiously. It might have been one of our storms back home in the north, though its wild refrains were sadder, more doleful.

You too are an exile, I thought. You mourn for the broad open steppes where you have room to spread your icy wings. Here you feel stifled and constricted, like an eagle that cries and beats against the bars of its iron cage.

'I don't like it,' said the captain. 'Look at it. You can't see a thing. Nothing but snow and mist. We'll be over a cliff or stuck in a gulley if we don't watch out. Then farther down we'll very likely find the Baidara in full spate, so we shan't get across. Asia! What a place! The people and the rivers are as bad as each other – there's no depending on 'em.'

The drivers shouted and swore as they whipped the horses,

which snorted and held back. They would not budge for anything, for all the eloquence of the whips.

At last one driver said:

'We'll never make Kobi today, sir. Shall we turn off to the
left while we still can? There's something over there on the
hillside. Must be huts. Travellers always put up here in bad
weather.' He pointed to an Ossete. 'They say they'll take us
there if you give them a tip.'

'I know, lad, I don't need you to tell me,' said the captain.
'Lord, what swine! They never miss a chance to pick up a tip.'

'Still, you must admit we'd be worse off without them,'
I said.

'I know, I know,' he muttered. 'Huh! Guides! They know
which side their bread's buttered. Making out you can't find
the way without them to help!'

So we turned off to the left and after a good deal of trouble
reached our humble shelter. It consisted of two huts built of flat
stones and rubble, enclosed by a wall of the same material. Our
ragged hosts gave us a warm welcome. I learnt afterwards that
they are paid and kept by the government on condition they
take in travellers caught by storms.

I sat down by the fire.

'It's all to the good,' I said. 'Now you can finish your story
about Bela. I'm sure that wasn't the end of it.'

'What makes you so sure?' asked the captain, winking and
smiling artfully.

'Why, it's not in the nature of things. An unusual beginning
must have an unusual end.'

'As a matter of fact you're right.'

'Good.'

'It's all very well for you to be pleased. It's sad for me,
though, to look back on it. She was a grand girl, was Bela.
I got so attached to her, I loved her like a daughter. She was

48

fond of me too. I have no family, you know. It's twelve years
or more since I heard anything of my father and mother. I never
thought of taking a wife earlier on and now at my age it
wouldn't be proper. So I was glad to have someone to make a
fuss of. She used to sing songs for us or dance the *lezginka*. Some
dancer she was too. I've seen our young ladies in the provinces,
and once, twenty years back, I even went to the Assembly
Rooms in Moscow – but those girls weren't a patch on Bela.
She was in a different class altogether. Pechorin dressed her up
like a doll, and it was amazing how much prettier she grew
while with us, with all his pampering and coddling. She lost the
sunburn on her face and arms and got some colour in her
cheeks. A gay spark she was, always teasing me, the little imp
. . . God forgive her.'

'And what happened when you told her her father was dead?'

'We kept it from her for a long time. Then when she was
used to being with us we told her. She cried for a couple of days,
then forgot all about it.

'Everything was fine for three or four months. I think I told
you Pechorin was very keen on hunting. He'd a regular passion
for it, always out in the forest after wild boar or goats. But now
he never so much as went outside the ramparts. Soon, though,
I saw he was brooding again, walking round the room with his
hands behind his back. Then one day he went off shooting
without saying a word to anybody. He was gone the whole
morning. It happened once, then again. Then more and more
often. Something's up, I thought. They've had a tiff.

'I went in to see them one morning. I can see it now – Bela
sitting on the bed in a black silk *beshmet* and looking that pale
and sad it gave me quite a turn.

'"Where's Pechorin?" I said.

'"Hunting."

'"Did he leave this morning?"

'She said nothing. She seemed to find it hard to talk. In the end she gave a deep sigh and said:

'"No, he went yesterday."

'"You don't suppose anything has happened to him?" I said.

'She answered through her tears.

'"All day yesterday I was thinking, imagining all kinds of accidents. One moment I thought he'd been wounded by a boar, then that he'd been carried off to the hills by some Chechen. But now I think he doesn't love me any more."

'"Truly, my dear, that's the worst possible thing you could think."

'She burst into tears. Then she proudly lifted her head and wiped her eyes.

'"If he doesn't love me," she said, "why can't he send me home? I'm not forcing him to keep me. I'll go myself if it goes on like this. I'm not his slave, I'm a chief's daughter."

'I tried to talk her round.

'"Look, Bela," I said. "You can't expect him to spend his whole time here tied to your apron-strings. He's a young man and fond of the chase. He'll go off hunting, then come back. But if you're going to mope, he'll soon get tired of you."

'"Yes, you're right," she said. "I'll cheer up."

'She laughed and took her tambourine and started to sing and dance and leap around me. But this didn't last long either. She fell on to the bed again and covered her face with her hands.

'What could I do with her? You see, I'd never had any truck with women. I racked my brains for some way of comforting her, but I couldn't think of anything. For some time neither of us spoke. Very awkward it was, I assure you.

'In the end I asked if she would like a walk to the ramparts, as the weather was fine. It was September and a really lovely day, bright but not too hot. The mountains all round were as clear as anything. We set off and walked along the ramparts for

a long time, saying nothing. At last she sat down on the grass
with me beside her. It's really funny to look back on – there was
I fussing over her like a nursemaid.

'Our fort stood on high ground, with a magnificent view
from the ramparts. On one side was a broad stretch of open
country with gullies running across it, and forest beyond
stretching right up to the mountains. Here and there you'd see
smoke from the villages, and herds of horses moving about. On
the other side there was a shallow stream, bordered by the
thick scrub of the stony mountains that link up with the main
Caucasus range.

'We sat on the corner of the bastion, with a good view in
both directions. Suddenly I saw a man on a grey horse coming
out of the wood. He came closer and closer, then stopped on the
far side of the stream a couple of hundred yards away. He was
wheeling his horse round like a madman. I couldn't understand
what he was up to.

'"Your eyes are younger than mine, Bela," I said. "Can you
see who that rider is? Who's he putting on that show for?"

'She had a look and shrieked:

'"It's Kazbich!"

'"The scoundrel!" I cried. "Come to make sport of us, has
he?"

'I had a good look. It was Kazbich sure enough, the black-
faced scoundrel, as tattered and filthy as ever.

'"That's my father's horse!" said Bela, grasping my arm.
She was trembling like a leaf, her eyes flashing.

'"Ho, ho!" I thought. "The brigand's blood's coming out
in you as well, my sweetheart!"

'I called the sentry.

'"Come here," I said. "Look your gun over and pick me off
that fellow down there. I'll give you a silver rouble if you do."

'"Very good, sir," says he. "But he don't keep still."

'"You tell him to," I laughed.

'So the sentry waved to him and shouted:

'"Hold still a minute, friend. What do you think you are, a top or something?"

'Kazbich stopped and listened – he must have thought we wanted to parley. But he had another think coming to him! My grenadier took aim and fired. He missed. The moment the powder flashed in the pan, Kazbich spurred his horse and it leapt to one side. He stood up in the stirrups and shouted something in his own language, then shook his whip at us and was gone.

'"You ought to be ashamed of yourself," I told the sentry.

'"He's gone off to die, sir," he said. "You can't kill these damned people straight off."

'A quarter of an hour later Pechorin came back from hunting. Bela threw her arms round his neck with never a murmur of complaint or reproach about his being away so long.

'Even I was annoyed with him.

'"Look here," I said. "Kazbich was just across the river a minute ago and we took a shot at him. You might easily have bumped into him. These hillmen don't take things lying down. He must have guessed you had a hand in helping Azamat, and I don't mind betting he recognized Bela just now. He was very keen on her a year ago – I know that for a fact, for he told me so himself. If he'd seen his way to raising the bride-money, he'd have asked for her hand, for sure."

'This made Pechorin think.

'"Yes," he said. "We must be more careful. Bela, from now on you must never go out on the ramparts again."

'I had a long talk with him that evening. It vexed me to see the way he'd changed towards the poor girl. Apart from spending half his time out hunting, he treated her coldly now and rarely made a fuss of her. You could see she was beginning to pine. Her face was drawn and she'd lost the sparkle in her big eyes. I'd say to her: "What are you sighing for, Bela? Feeling sad?" "No," she'd say. "Is there something you want?" "No." "Feeling homesick?" "I haven't got a home." Sometimes you'd get nothing out of her for days on end but just "Yes" and "No".

'This was what I talked to Pechorin about.

'"Look, Maxim Maximych," he said. "I've got an unfortunate character. I don't know how I came by it, whether it was the way I was brought up or whether it's just the way I'm made. All I know is that if I make other people unhappy, I'm no less unhappy myself. Not much comfort for them perhaps, but there it is. As a young man, as soon as I got my freedom I threw myself wildly into all the pleasures that money can buy, and soon got tired of them, needless to say. Then I went in for society high-life and before long I was tired of that too. I fell in love with women of fashion and was loved in return. But their love merely stirred my imagination and vanity, my heart remained empty. I took to reading and study, but grew tired of that too. I saw I had no need of learning to win fame or happiness, for the happiest people are the ignoramuses, and fame is a matter of luck and you only need to be smart to get it. I got bored after that.

'"After a while I was posted to the Caucasus. That was the happiest time in my life. I hoped there'd be an end to boredom with Chechen bullets flying around, but I was wrong. After a month I was so used to the hum of bullets and to being close to death that I honestly took more notice of the mosquitoes. Now I was more bored than ever, with just about my last hope gone. When I saw Bela in my quarters and held her on my knees and kissed her black curls for the first time I was silly enough to think she was an angel sent down to me by a merciful fate. I was wrong again. A native girl's love is little better than that of a lady of rank. The ignorance and simplicity of the one are as tiresome as the coquetry of the other. If you like, I'm still in love with her. I'm grateful to her for a few moments of relative bliss. I'd give my life for her. But she bores me. I don't know whether I'm a fool or a scoundrel, but one thing I am sure of is that I'm just as much to be pitied as she is, perhaps even more. My soul's been corrupted by society. My imagination knows no peace, my heart no satisfaction. I'm never satisfied. I grow used to sorrow as easily as I do to pleasure, and my life gets emptier every day. The only thing left for me is to travel. As soon as I can I'll leave. Not for Europe, though, not on your life. I'll go to America, Arabia, India. With luck I'll die somewhere on the way. At least I can be sure that with storms and bad roads to help this final solace will last me a while."

'He talked a long time in this vein. What he said made a deep impression on me, for it was the first time I'd ever heard such things from a man of twenty-five, and God grant it may be the last. It's quite beyond me. Now you're a man who's lately been in the capital,' he said, looking at me. 'Is it true that all the young people there are the same?'

I said there were a lot of people who did talk like that and very likely some of them told the truth, but disenchantment, like any other fashion, having started off among the élite had now been passed down to finish its days among the lower orders. I explained that now the people who suffered most from boredom tried to keep their misfortune to themselves, as if it were some vice.

The captain could not understand these subtleties. He shook his head.

'I suppose it was the French who started this fashion of being bored?' he said, smiling artfully.

'No, the English.'

'Aha, so that's it! They always were a drunken lot,' he retorted. I could not help recalling the Moscow lady who used to

maintain that Byron was no more than a drunkard. But the
captain had more excuse for talking this way, since, being
anxious to keep off alcohol, he naturally tried to persuade himself that drunkenness was the root of all evil.

Meanwhile he continued his story.

'Kazbich didn't show up again. Still, for some reason I
couldn't get rid of the idea that he'd come for a purpose and
was up to some devilry.

'One day Pechorin tried to get me to go boar-hunting with
him. I put him off for a long time – really, as if I cared about
wild boar! But in the end he got me to go with him, and we set
off first thing in the morning with half a dozen soldiers. We
routed about in the forest and among the reeds till ten o'clock,
but found no boar.

'"We may as well go back," I said. "What's the point of
keeping on? It's plain we're out of luck today."

'But Pechorin wasn't for going back empty-handed, no
matter how tired we were. He was like that. He'd get something into his head and not be content till he got it. He must
have been spoilt as a child. At midday we did at last come on a
confounded boar and got in a couple of shots, but it was no
good – he got away among the reeds. It just wasn't our day. So
we had a bit of a rest and set off home.

'We rode side by side in silence, trailing our reins, and we'd
almost reached the fort – it was just out of sight behind some
bushes – when we heard a shot. We looked at each other, both
seized with the same suspicion, and galloped full tilt to where
the shot had come from. We saw a group of soldiers gathered
on the ramparts and pointing out across the plain. There was a
horseman going like the wind, with something white across the
saddle. Pechorin let out a shriek as good as any Chechen,
grabbed his gun from the holster and was after him like a shot,
with me following behind.

'As luck had it, our horses were still fresh, as we'd seen little sport, and they went flat out. Every second we got closer. Then at last I saw it was Kazbich, though I couldn't make out what he was holding in front of him. I came level with Pechorin and shouted to him that it was Kazbich. He glanced at me, nodded and whipped up his horse.

'At length we got within range. Perhaps Kazbich's horse was tired or just not as good as ours, anyway despite his efforts it made little headway. I fancy Kazbich must have spared a thought for his Karagyoz just then.

'I saw Pechorin take aim at the gallop. "Don't fire," I shouted. "Save your shot. We'll catch him anyway." But young people are all the same – they always get excited at the wrong moment. There was a shot, and the bullet got Kazbich's horse in the back leg. In the heat of the moment it bounded on another dozen steps, then stumbled and fell on its knees. Kazbich jumped off and we saw then that he was carrying a woman wrapped in a *yashmak*. It was Bela, poor thing.

'Kazbich shouted something to us in his own language and lifted a dagger over her. There was no time to waste. I fired my shot without taking aim and must have got him in the shoulder, for suddenly he dropped his arm. When the smoke cleared I saw the wounded horse lying on the ground with Bela by its side. Kazbich had thrown away his gun and was scrambling like a cat through the bushes up a crag. I'd have liked to bring him down from there, but my gun needed reloading. We jumped off our horses and rushed to Bela. Poor soul, she lay quite still, with blood streaming from her wound. That devil Kazbich couldn't stab her clean in the heart and get it over with, he had to stab her in the back like the dirty scoundrel he was.

'She was unconscious. We tore up her *yashmak* and tied up the wound as tight as we could. Pechorin kissed her cold lips in vain. Nothing could bring her round.

'Pechorin mounted while I lifted her up and somehow we managed to get her on to his saddle. He put his arms round her and we started back. We said nothing for a few minutes, then Pechorin spoke.

'"Look, Maxim Maximych, we'll never get her back alive like this."

'I agreed, so we galloped as fast as we could go. There was a crowd to meet us at the fort gate. We carried her carefully across to Pechorin's quarters and sent for the doctor, who was drunk, but came just the same. He looked at the wound and said she wouldn't last more than a day. He was wrong, though . . .'

'Did she get better then?' I asked the captain, seizing him by the arm. I could not help being pleased.

'No,' he said. 'The doctor was wrong because in fact she lived for two days.'

'How did Kazbich manage to get her away then?' I asked.

'It was like this. Although Pechorin had told her not to, she went out of the fort down to the stream. It was very hot, you see, so she sat down on a stone and dangled her feet in the water. Kazbich sneaked up, grabbed her, put his hand over her mouth and pulled her into the bushes. Then he was up in the saddle and off. She meantime managed to let out a shout and rouse the sentries. They fired, but missed, and that's when we turned up.'

'But why did Kazbich want to take her away?'

'Why, what do you think? These Circassians have got thieving in their blood. They'll steal anything, given the chance. Even things they don't want – they'll take them just the same. They just can't help it. And besides he'd long had a fancy for her.'

'Bela died then?'

'Yes, she died, though the agony lasted a long time. It was

pretty agonizing for us too. About ten that evening she came round. We sat by her bed. The moment she opened her eyes she called for Pechorin.

'"I'm here by your side, my *dzhanechka* (my darling, that is),' he said and took her hand.

'"I'm going to die," she said.

'We comforted her, told her the doctor had promised to make her better without fail, but she shook her head and turned to the wall. She didn't want to die.

'In the night she became delirious. Her head was burning and every so often her whole body shook with fever. She rambled on about her father and her brother, and said she wanted to go home to the mountains. Then she talked about Pechorin too, called him all kinds of affectionate names or else reproached him for no longer loving his *dzhanechka*.

'He listened to her, without a word, resting his head on his hands. All this time, though, I never once saw a tear in his eye. Perhaps he couldn't cry, perhaps he controlled himself, I don't know. As far as I was concerned, I'd never seen anything so pathetic in my life.

'By morning the delirium had passed. She lay still for an hour or so. She was pale and so weak you could hardly tell she was breathing. Then she improved and started talking. Do you know what about? It was the kind of fancy that only comes to people when they are dying. She said she felt sad that she wasn't a Christian and that her spirit would never meet Pechorin's in the next world and some other woman would be his sweetheart in heaven. I thought of getting her baptized before she died and suggested it to her. She looked at me, not sure what to do. She couldn't speak for a long time, but in the end said she'd die in the faith she'd been born in.

'The whole day passed like this. What a change came over her in that one day! Her cheeks were pale and sunken, her eyes enormous, her lips afire. She had a burning pain, like a red hot iron in her breast.

'The next night came. We never shut an eye and stayed by her bed the whole time. She was groaning and in terrible agony. When the pain let up she tried to make Pechorin think she felt better, told him to go to bed, kissed his hand and wouldn't let it go.

'Just before dawn the death agony started. She tossed and turned, the bandage came off and she started bleeding again. We tied up the wound and she was quiet for a minute and asked Pechorin to kiss her. He knelt by the bed, raised her head from the pillow and pressed his lips to hers, from which the warmth was already passing. She hugged him tight round the neck, her arms trembling, as though she was trying to pass her soul to him with that kiss. No, it was right and proper she should die! What would have become of her if Pechorin had left her, as he would have done sooner or later?

'Half the next day she was quiet, saying nothing, and doing all she was told, however much the doctor tormented her with his poultices and medicine.

'"Look here," I told him. "You said yourself she's bound to die, so why bother with all these concoctions of yours?"

'"It's better this way," he says. "I must keep a clear conscience."

'Conscience, my foot!

'In the afternoon she felt thirsty. We opened the window, but it was hotter outside than in. We put ice by the bed, but it was no use. I knew this frantic thirst was a sign that the end was near and told Pechorin so. Bela raised herself on the bed and called out hoarsely for water. Pechorin turned white as a sheet, snatched up a glass, poured some water and gave it her. I put my hands over my eyes and said a prayer, which one I don't remember. Yes, sir, I've seen plenty of people dying in hospitals and on the battlefield, but this was something different, altogether different. Truth to tell, it still grieves me that she never once remembered me as she lay dying, though I think I loved her like a father. Well, God forgive her ... And after all, who am I that people should think of me when they're dying?

'The moment she drank the water she felt better, but then two or three minutes later she passed away. We put a mirror to her lips and it didn't blur. I took Pechorin out of the room and we went to the ramparts. We walked up and down for a long time, our hands behind our backs, saying nothing. His face showed nothing in particular, and that annoyed me. If I'd been in his place I'd have died of grief. In the end he sat on the ground in some shade and started drawing in the sand with a stick. I wanted to console him, more for decency's sake, you understand, than anything else. But when I spoke he lifted up his head and laughed. That laugh sent cold shivers down my spine.

'I went off to order the coffin. I confess it was partly to occupy my mind that I saw to this. I lined the coffin with a piece of Persian silk I had and trimmed it round with some silver Circassian lace that Pechorin had bought for Bela.

'Early next morning we buried her where she had last sat, outside the fort by the stream. White acacias and elder have grown up round her grave now. I wanted to put up a cross, but didn't like to somehow. After all, she wasn't a Christian.'

'What about Pechorin?' I asked.

'Poor chap. He was out of sorts for a long time and got very thin. But we never talked of Bela after that. I could see it would upset him, so what was the point? Three or four months later he was posted to another regiment and went off to Georgia, and I've not heard of him since then. I seem to remember somebody told me recently he'd gone back to Russia, though there was nothing about it in divisional orders. But then, we're always the last to get the news.'

At this point he launched into a lengthy discourse on the inconveniences of hearing news a year after the event. Probably he wanted to forget his sad memories. I did not interrupt him, nor did I listen.

In an hour it was possible to move on. The storm had abated, the sky had cleared, and we set off. As we journeyed I could not help bringing up the subject of Bela and Pechorin again.

'Did you never hear what happened to Kazbich?' I asked.

'Kazbich? No, I don't rightly know. I've heard tell the Shapsugs have got a daredevil fellow called Kazbich on their right flank – he wears a red *beshmet*, and whenever he comes under our fire he just walks his horse up and down, and bows nicely every time a bullet whistles by. But it can hardly be the same one.'

At Kobi, Maxim Maximych and I parted company. I travelled on by post chaise, and he, with his heavy luggage, could not keep up with me. We never expected to meet again, but in fact we did. If you like I will tell you about it – it is quite a story. Don't you agree, though, that Maxim Maximych is a sterling fellow? If you do, then I shall be amply rewarded for my – perhaps too lengthy – tale.

II
MAXIM MAXIMYCH

AFTER leaving Maxim Maximych I travelled briskly through the Terek and Daryal gorges, lunched at Kazbek, had tea at Lars and arrived in Vladikavkaz in time for supper. But I won't burden you with descriptions of mountains, meaningless exclamations of rapture, depictions of scenery which convey nothing, least of all to anyone who has never been there, and statistics which no one would ever read.

I put up at the hotel where travellers always stay and where, I might mention, it's impossible to get a pheasant roasted or a drop of soup cooked, because the three old soldiers in charge of it are too stupid or too drunk to do a thing.

I was told I would have to spend another three days there since the 'detachment' had not yet arrived from Yekaterinograd and was therefore in no position to return. I did not view that with detachment! However, a bad pun is small comfort for a Russian, and I decided to pass the time by writing down Maxim Maximych's story of Bela. Little did I think it would be the first of a whole series of tales. It just goes to show what terrible consequences a trivial incident can have.

But you may not know what a 'detachment' is? It is an escort – half a company of infantry and one cannon – that accompanies convoys passing through Kabarda on their way from Vladikavkaz to Yekaterinograd.

My first day there was very tedious. Early next morning a cart drove into the yard, and who should it be but Maxim Maximych! We greeted each other like long lost friends. I gave him the use of my room. He did not stand on ceremony and even went so far as to slap me on the back and curl his lips in an apology for a smile. What a strange fellow he is!

Maxim Maximych was well versed in the culinary arts and produced a remarkably good roast pheasant, nicely topped with a cucumber sauce. I must admit that but for him I should have had to make do with hard tack. A bottle of Kakhetian wine helped us to forget the modest number of courses (one in all), and after dinner we lit our pipes and settled ourselves, I by the window, Maxim Maximych by the stove, which had been lit as the day was damp and cold.

We sat in silence. What was there to talk about? He had already told me all there was of interest and I, for my part, had nothing to tell. I looked out of the window. Through the trees I glimpsed numerous small houses dotted along the bank of the Terek, which gets steadily wider all the time. Beyond lay the jagged blue wall of mountains, with the white cardinal's cap of Kazbek peeping out behind. I was sorry to be leaving them and bade them a mental farewell.

We sat like this for a long time. The sun dipped behind the cold mountain peaks and a whitish mist began to spread through the valleys. Suddenly there was the sound of a carriage bell and the shout of coachmen outside. Some carts of filthy Armenians drove into the hotel yard, followed by an empty calash. Its light wheels, comfortable fittings and modish appearance had a foreign stamp about them. A servant walked behind. He wore large mustachios and a braided jacket and was rather well-dressed for a servant, but the devil-may-care flourish with which he knocked out his pipe and the way he shouted at the driver left one in no doubt as to his station in life. He was clearly the pampered servant of a lazy master, a kind of Russian Figaro. I called to him from the window.

'I say, my man! Is that the detachment arrived?'

He gave me a rather insolent look, straightened his neckband

and turned away. An Armenian walking beside him smiled and answered for him. It was the detachment, he said, and it would be going back the next morning.

'Thank heavens for that!' said Maxim Maximych, who had joined me at the window. 'Why, that's a mighty fine carriage!' he added. 'Must be some official on his way to Tiflis for an inquiry. You can see he doesn't know much about the hills in these parts. They're cruel they are, make no mistake. Even an English carriage wouldn't stand up to them.'

'I wonder who it can be,' I said. 'Let's go and find out.'

We went out into the passage. At the far end a door leading to a side room was open. The servant and the driver were carrying cases into it.

'Here, fellow!' said Maxim Maximych to the servant. 'Whose is that splendid calash out there, eh? It's a fine job.'

Without turning, the servant muttered something under his breath and went on untying a case. Maxim Maximych was annoyed and touched the churlish fellow on the shoulder.

'Here, I'm speaking to you, my man . . .' he said.

'Whose calash? It's my master's.'

'And who's your master?'

'Pechorin . . .'

'What's that? Pechorin? Why, good heavens above!' exclaimed Maxim Maximych, tugging my sleeve. 'Did your master ever see service in the Caucasus?' he asked, his eyes shining with joy.

'Yes, I think he did. I've not been with him long,' said the servant.

'That's it, that's it! Grigory Alexandrovich – that's his name, isn't it? I was a friend of your master's,' he said, giving the servant a friendly slap on the shoulder that sent him staggering.

The servant frowned.

'If you please, sir. You're holding me up,' he said.

'Heavens above, fellow! You don't seem to realize – we were bosom pals, your master and I. Shared quarters, we did. But where's your master got to?'

The servant explained that Pechorin was dining and spending the night at the house of Colonel N.

'Do you think he'll be coming round here this evening?' asked Maxim Maximych. 'Or perhaps you'll have to go and see him about something? If you do, tell him Maxim Maximych is here. Just say that, he'll know. . . . There'll be an eighty-copek piece for you.'

The servant gave a look of disdain on hearing this modest promise. Still, he told Maxim Maximych he would do as he asked.

'You see. He'll be round at once,' Maxim Maximych told me with a triumphant look. 'I'll go and wait for him outside the gate. What a nuisance it is I don't know N.'

Maxim Maximych sat down on the bench outside the gate and I went back to my room. I must confess I was also rather keen to see this man Pechorin. The impression I had gained of him from the captain's story was not a specially favourable one, but some features of his character had struck me as remarkable.

An hour passed. One of the old soldiers brought in a boiling *samovar* and a teapot.

I shouted to Maxim Maximych out of the window.

'Maxim Maximych! Will you have some tea?'

'No, thanks very much,' he said. 'I don't feel like any just now.'

'Come on, have some. The time's getting on, and it's chilly.'

'I'm all right, thanks very much.'

'Very well. Please yourself.'

I started on the tea by myself. Ten minutes later in came my old friend.

'You're right,' he said. 'A drop of tea would be best, after all. I've been waiting all this time. His servant went to see him a long time ago, but he must have got held up.'

He quickly gulped down a cup of tea, refused a second and went off to the gate again, looking upset. He was clearly hurt by Pechorin's indifference, particularly as he had just been telling me what great friends they were and an hour ago had been sure Pechorin would rush to see him at the mere mention of his name.

It was already late and dark when I next opened the window and called Maxim Maximych to tell him it was bedtime. He muttered something through his teeth, and when I repeated the invitation he made no reply.

I left a candle on the bench by the stove, wrapped myself in my greatcoat and lay down on the couch. I soon dozed off and would have slept peacefully through till morning, if Maxim Maximych had not woken me. He came in very late, threw his pipe on the table, paced up and down the room, tinkered with the stove, and when he finally did go to bed, he coughed, spat and tossed and turned for a long time.

'Bedbugs troubling you?' I asked.

He gave a deep sigh.

'Yes, that's it,' he said.

I woke early in the morning, but Maxim Maximych was up before me. I found him sitting on the bench by the gate.

'I've got to call on the commandant,' he said. 'So would you send round for me if Pechorin turns up?'

I said I would, and he ran off as though his limbs had regained all the vigour and litheness of youth.

It was a beautiful morning, though fresh. Golden clouds massed on the mountains like some new range of aerial peaks. Outside the gate there was a broad square, with a market on the far side. As it was Sunday the market was bustling with people, and barefooted Ossete boys swarmed round me with baskets of honeycombs on their backs. I sent them packing. I had other thoughts, for I was beginning to share the concern of the good captain.

Within ten minutes the man we awaited appeared at the end of the square with Colonel N. The colonel accompanied him as far as the hotel, then said good-bye and walked off towards the fort. I at once sent one of the old soldiers to fetch Maxim Maximych.

Pechorin's servant came out of the hotel to meet him. He said that the horses would be harnessed at once and handed him a cigar-box. Pechorin gave some instructions and the servant went off to attend to them. His master lit a cigar, yawned a couple of times and sat down on the bench on the far side of the gate.

I must now give you a portrait of him.

He was of average height, with broad shoulders and a slender shapely figure that indicated a strong physique, capable of enduring the rigours of a life spent travelling in different climates, and proof against the turmoil of passions and the dissoluteness of city life. His dusty velvet coat was undone, except for the two bottom buttons, and an expanse of dazzling white linen showed him to be a man of refined habits. His stained gloves might have been made for his small aristocratic hands, and when he took one off I was astonished to see the slenderness of his pale fingers. He had a casual, indolent walk, and I noticed that he did not swing his arms – a sure sign of reserve in a man. However, these are personal views based on my own observations and I have no wish to force them on other people.

When Pechorin sat down on the bench his erect figure bent as though he hadn't a bone in his back. His whole posture gave the impression of nervous exhaustion. He sat in the manner of

Balzac's *femme de trente ans* sitting in her cushioned armchair at the end of a fatiguing ball. On first seeing his face I would have thought him no older than twenty-three, though later I would have taken him for thirty. There was something childlike in the way he smiled. His skin was delicate, like a woman's, and his naturally curly fair hair made a fine setting for the pale, noble brow. Only a prolonged scrutiny of his forehead revealed traces of criss-cross wrinkles that probably showed up much more in moments of anger or stress. Though his hair was fair, his moustache and eyebrows were black. In a man this is as sure a sign of breeding as a black mane and tail are in a grey horse. I will finish my portrait by noting his slightly turned-up nose, brilliant white teeth and brown eyes.

I must say a little more about his eyes. In the first place, they never laughed when he laughed. Have you ever noticed this peculiarity some people have? It is either the sign of an evil nature or of a profound and lasting sorrow. His eyes shone beneath his half-lowered lids with a kind of phosphorescent brilliance (if one can put it like that). This brilliance was not the outward sign of an ardent spirit or a lively imagination. It was like the cold dazzling brilliance of smooth steel. When he looked at you, his quick, penetrating, sombre glance left you with the unpleasant feeling that you'd been asked an indiscreet question. It would have seemed insolent, if it hadn't been so calm and indifferent.

All these thoughts may have suggested themselves to me merely because I knew something of his life, and possibly he would have made an entirely different impression on someone else. Still, as you will hear nothing of Pechorin except from me, you must be content with the picture I give you. Let me conclude by saying that he was on the whole rather good-looking, with one of those unusual faces that appeal particularly to society women.

The horses were already harnessed. There was an occasional tinkle from the bell under the bow of the harness-frame. Twice Pechorin's servant came up to announce that all was ready, and still there was no sign of Maxim Maximych. Luckily, Pechorin seemed to be in no hurry to be off. He sat lost in thought, gazing at the jagged blue outline of the Caucasus. I went up to him and said:

'If you'd care to wait a little longer you'll have the pleasure of meeting an old friend.'

'Ah, that's right,' he answered hastily. 'I was told about him yesterday. But where is he?'

I turned towards the square and saw Maxim Maximych running as fast as his legs could carry him. In a few minutes he was with us, gasping for breath, the sweat pouring from his face. Strands of wet grey hair sticking out from his cap clung to his brow. His knees were shaking. He was about to throw his arms round Pechorin, but Pechorin rather coldly held out his hand, although he gave him a friendly smile. For a moment the captain was too taken aback to do anything, but then eagerly grasped Pechorin's hand with both his own. He was still unable to speak.

'Delighted to see you, dear Maxim Maximych,' said Pechorin. 'How are you?'

'And you, what about you?' the old man mumbled, with tears in his eyes, put out by Pechorin's formal tone. 'It's been a long time. . . . Where are you heading now?'

'Persia. Then on from there.'

'But you're not going this minute, are you? My dear fellow, you must stay on for a bit. We can't part straight away after not seeing each other all this time.'

'I must be going, Maxim Maximych,' replied Pechorin.

'But merciful heavens, man, what's all the rush? I've got so many things to tell you. And a lot of things to ask as well. How is it then? Left the army, have you? What have you been doing?'

Pechorin smiled.

'Being bored,' he said.

'Do you remember when we were at the fort together? Grand hunting country that! You were a keen shot too, weren't you. And do you remember Bela?'

Pechorin went a shade paler and turned away.

'Yes, I remember,' he said, and almost at once gave an affected yawn.

Maxim Maximych tried to persuade him to stay on for a couple of hours.

'We'll have a splendid dinner,' he said. 'I've got a couple of pheasants with me, and there's a fine Kakhetian wine here, not like you get in Georgia, of course, but first-class stuff. . . . We'll have a talk. You can tell me what you've been doing in Petersburg. How about it?'

'My dear Maxim Maximych, I've really nothing to tell. Well, good-bye. I really must be going – I'm in a hurry.' He took his hand. 'Good of you to remember me.'

The old man frowned. He was upset and annoyed, though he tried to hide it.

'Remember?' he growled. 'There's nothing wrong with *my* memory. Well, go your way then. I never thought we'd meet like this.'

Pechorin gave him a friendly hug.

'There now,' he said. 'I've not really changed, have I? But what can you do? We've all got our own way to go in life. Perhaps we'll meet again – who knows?'

As he said this he was already seated in the calash and the driver was gathering up the reins. Suddenly Maxim Maximych grabbed hold of the carriage door.

'Hey, wait a minute!' he shouted. 'I nearly forgot – I've

got those papers you left behind. I've been carting them round with me. I thought I might come across you in Georgia, but now I've run into you here. So what shall I do with them?'

'Whatever you like,' said Pechorin. 'Good-bye.'

Maxim Maximych shouted after him:

'You're off to Persia then? When'll you be back?'

The carriage was already far away, but Pechorin gave a wave with his hand, as much as to say 'Probably never. What's there to come back for?'

Long after the jingle of the harness-bell and the rumble of the wheels over the stony road had faded poor old Maxim Maximych still stood there, deep in thought. At length, trying hard to look indifferent, despite the tears of vexation that glistened on his eyelashes, he said:

'We used to be friends, of course. But what's friendship these days? Why should he bother with me? I'm not rich or important, am I? And anyway, I'm old enough to be his father. Did you see what a dandy he is now he's been back in Petersburg? How about that calash? And all that luggage, eh? And that stuck-up servant!'

He said this with a sarcastic smile. Then he turned to me.

'Tell me,' he said. 'What do you think? What on earth does he want to go off to Persia for? It's queer, it really is. I always knew he was flighty, of course, not the sort you can rely on. A pity he's got to come to a bad end, though. But it's bound to happen. As I've always said, no good ever comes of a man who forgets an old friend.'

He turned away to hide his feelings, then walked round his cart in the yard, pretending to inspect the wheels, though there were tears welling in his eyes. I went up to him.

'Maxim Maximych,' I said. 'What are those papers Pechorin left you?'

'Heaven knows. Notes of some kind.'

'What are you going to do with them?'

'Me? Why, use them for cartridge wads, I suppose.'

'Why not give them to me instead?'

He looked at me in astonishment. Then growling some incoherent remark, he began rummaging through his valise. He pulled out a notebook and tossed it disdainfully on the ground. A second, a third were treated in similar fashion till there were ten in all. There was something childish in his being so cross. I was amused, yet felt sorry for him too.

'That's the lot,' he said. 'I wish you joy of them.'

'Can I do what I like with them?' I asked.

'Print them in the papers for all I care. It's no concern of mine. I'm not a friend of his am I, or a relation? True, we lived a good while under the same roof – but then I've lived with plenty of different people in my time.'

I snatched up the papers and carried them off in case the captain should regret his decision. Soon afterwards we were told the detachment would be leaving in an hour and I ordered the horses to be harnessed. I was already putting on my cap when Maxim Maximych came into the room. He did not look as though he was getting ready to leave. There was an unnatural, cold air about him.

'What, aren't you going then?' I asked him.

'No.'

'Why ever not?'

'I've not seen the commandant yet, and I've got some government property to hand in.'

'But you've been to see him,' I said.

'Yes, I did go,' he stammered. 'He was out and . . . I didn't wait.'

I realized what he meant. Perhaps for the first time in his life the poor old fellow had neglected his duty 'in pursuit of personal ends' (as the official phrase goes) – and small thanks had he got for it.

'Maxim Maximych, I'm very sorry we're parting sooner than we'd thought,' I said.

'How can an ignorant old man like me keep up with you? You young society chaps, you're too stuck-up. As long as you're down here, with Circassian bullets flying round, you put up with fellows like me, but then you meet us afterwards and won't as much as offer your hand.'

'Maxim Maximych,' I said. 'I've done nothing to deserve these reproaches.'

'Oh, I was just speaking generally. No, I wish you luck and a pleasant journey.'

We said good-bye rather stiffly. Good kindly Maxim Maximych was now the pig-headed, crotchety captain. And the reason? All because Pechorin had without thinking, or for some other reason, offered his hand when Maxim Maximych had wanted to embrace him. It is sad to see a young man's fondest hopes and dreams shattered when the rose-coloured veil is plucked away and he sees the actions and feelings of men for what they are. But he still has the hope of replacing his old illusions with others, just as fleeting, but also just as sweet. But what can replace them in a man of Maxim Maximych's age? Inevitably, he becomes crusty and withdrawn.

I left alone.

PECHORIN'S JOURNAL

Foreword

NOT long ago I heard that Pechorin had died on his way back from Persia. I was delighted, since it means that I can print his notes, and I readily take this opportunity of putting my own name to somebody else's work. I only hope the reader won't blame me for this innocent deception.

I must now give some explanation of what prompted me to publish the innermost secrets of a man I never knew. It would have been different if I had been his friend, for we all know how treacherously indiscreet a true friend can be. But I only saw him once, and that in passing, so I cannot feel for him that inexpressible hatred which lurks beneath the mask of friendship and waits only for the death or downfall of the other in order to shower him with reproaches, advice, taunts and regrets.

Reading over these notes again, I felt convinced of the sincerity of the man who so ruthlessly exposed his own failings and vices. The story of a man's soul, however trivial, can be more interesting and instructive than the story of a whole nation, especially if it is based on the self-analysis of a mature mind and is written with no vain desire to rouse our sympathy or curiosity. The trouble with Rousseau's *Confessions* is that he read them to his friends.

It is only from a wish to be of service that I am publishing these extracts from a journal which came into my possession by chance. I have changed all the names, but the people mentioned in it will probably recognize themselves. They may also find some excuse for things done by this man (now no longer of this world), for which they censured him at the time – we practically always excuse things when we understand them.

In this book I have included only the parts about Pechorin's life in the Caucasus, though I have another thick notebook in which Pechorin gives his whole life-story. Some day that too will be put before the public, but there are a number of important reasons why I cannot undertake this at the moment.

Some readers might like to know my own opinion of Pechorin's character. My answer is given in the title of this book. 'Malicious irony!' they'll retort. I don't know.

TAMAN

TAMAN is the foulest hole among all the sea-coast towns of Russia. I practically starved to death there, then on top of that someone tried to drown me. I arrived there late one night by stage. The driver pulled up the weary *troika* by the gate of the one stone house in the place, just at the entrance to the town. Hearing the harness-bell, a Black Sea Cossack sentry gave a wild yell, half-asleep: 'Who goes there?' A Cossack sergeant and corporal came out. I explained I was an officer travelling on duty to my unit at the front and wanted a billet for the night. The corporal took us round the town. Every house we stopped at was full. I'd had no sleep for three nights and was tired and cold. I began to lose my temper. 'Take me anywhere, damn you!' I shouted. 'To the devil himself, as long as it's a place to sleep.' The corporal scratched the back of his head. 'There is one other place, sir, but you wouldn't fancy it. Unwholesome, it is.'

I didn't know what he meant by this last remark and told him to lead the way. We passed through a lot of filthy back-streets, seeing nothing but ramshackle fences, till finally we drove up to a small hut right on the edge of the sea.

A full moon shone on the thatched roof and white walls of my new abode. The yard had a rubble wall round it, and in the yard was another tumbledown shack, smaller and more ancient than the first. Almost at the foot of its walls there was a sheer drop to the sea, with dark blue waves splashing and murmuring unceasingly below. The moon looked calmly down on the turbulent element it ruled. Some way off shore I could make out two ships in the moonlight, their black rigging motionless, silhouetted like a spider's web against the pale outline of the horizon. There are ships at the quay, so I can leave for Gelenjik tomorrow, I thought.

My batman was a Cossack from one of the frontier regiments. I told him to get my valise down and dismiss the driver, then called for the master of the house. There was no answer. I knocked, and still there was no answer. What did it mean?

In the end a boy of about fourteen came out from the porch.

'Where's the master?' I asked.

'No master here,' answered the boy in Ukrainian.

'You mean there isn't a master at all?'

'That's right.'

'Well, where's the mistress?'

'Gone to the village.'

'Who'll open the door for me then?' I asked, giving it a kick. The door opened by itself, and a dank smell came from within. I lit a sulphur match and held it up to the boy's face. Its light showed a pair of wall-eyes: the boy was totally blind, and had been since birth. He stood before me without moving, and I had a good look at his face.

I confess I'm strongly prejudiced against the blind, one-eyed, deaf, dumb, legless, armless, hunch-backed, and so on. I've noticed there's always some odd link between a person's outward appearance and his inner self, as though when a man loses a limb he loses some inner feeling as well.

So I studied the blind boy's face. But what can you expect to see in a face without eyes? I took a long look at him, and couldn't help feeling sorry for him, when suddenly the ghost of a smile flitted across his thin lips. For some reason this struck me very unpleasantly. I had an idea that this blind boy might not be so blind as he seemed. I told myself that there was no way of faking wall-eyes, and anyway why should he want to? But it was no good – prejudice often takes me this way.

In the end I said:

'You the son of the house?'

'No.'

'Who are you then?'

'A poor orphan.'

'Has the woman got any children?'

'No. She had a daughter, but she went off with a Tatar. Over the sea.'

'Who was this Tatar?'

'I don't know. A Crimean Tatar he was, a boatman from Kerch.'

I went into the hut. There was no furniture apart from a table, a couple of benches and a huge chest by the stove. There wasn't a single icon on the walls – a bad sign. The sea wind blew through a broken window-pane.

I took a stump of candle from my valise, lit it and unpacked. I stood my sabre and gun in the corner, laid my pistols on the table and spread my cape out on one of the benches, while my Cossack did the same on the other. Ten minutes later he was snoring, but I couldn't get to sleep. I kept seeing the wall-eyed boy before me in the darkness.

An hour or so passed. The moonlight shining through the window played on the mud floor of the hut. Suddenly a shadow flitted across the patch of moonlight on the floor. I sat up and looked at the window. Once more someone ran past it and vanished. I couldn't imagine that this person had run on down the vertical drop to the sea, but there was nowhere else he could have gone.

I got up, put on my *beshmet*, fastened my belt and dagger and crept silently out of the hut. Coming towards me was the blind boy. I hid by the fence and he walked past me, his step cautious, but sure. He had a bundle under his arm. Turning towards the quay, he started down the steep and narrow pathway. Then shall the dumb sing and the blind see, I thought, and went after him, keeping close enough to have him in sight.

By now the moon was clouding over. A mist lay over the sea, and the stern lantern of the nearest ship glimmered faintly through it. Foaming breakers gleamed along the shore, threatening every minute to overwhelm it.

I made my way with difficulty down the steep slope and saw the blind boy pause at the bottom and turn right along the foot of the cliff. He walked very close to the water's edge and looked every moment as though he would be swept away by a wave. But judging by the sureness with which he jumped from rock to rock, avoiding the hollows, it was clearly not the first time he had taken this walk.

In the end he stopped and sat down on the beach, placing his bundle beside him and apparently listening for something. I watched his movements from behind a protruding rock. In a few minutes a white figure appeared from the other direction. It came up to the blind boy and sat down beside him. The wind brought me snatches of their conversation.

'What do you think, blind boy?' said a woman's voice. 'It's very rough. Yanko won't come.'

'Yanko's not afraid of storms,' said the blind boy.

'The mist's thickening,' said the woman, a note of sadness in her voice.

'It's easier to slip past the coastguards when it's misty,' replied the boy.

'And what if he's drowned?'

'What if he is? You'll go to church on Sunday without a new ribbon.'

There was silence. One thing had struck me, though – when the blind boy had talked to me he had spoken Ukrainian, but now he spoke pure Russian.

'There, I was right,' said the blind boy, clapping his hands.

'Yanko's not afraid of sea or wind or mist or coastguards. Listen! That's not the sea splashing – it's Yanko's long oars. You can't fool me.'

The woman leapt up and peered anxiously out to sea.

'Rubbish,' she said. 'I can't see anything.'

I looked hard out to sea, but I must say I could see nothing like a boat. Ten minutes went by, then, suddenly, a black speck appeared among the mountainous waves. One moment it grew bigger, the next smaller, rising slowly on the crests and dropping swiftly into the troughs of the waves. It was a boat coming in to shore. It was a bold sailor indeed who ventured out across the fifteen miles of the straits on such a night. And he must have some very special reason for doing it.

Turning this over in my mind, I watched with bated breath as the frail little craft dived like a duck into the abyss, then, beating its oars like wings, rose up again in a shower of spray. Next I thought it was going to be dashed to pieces on the shore, but it deftly turned broadside and slipped unscathed into the tiny bay.

Out of it stepped a man of middle height, wearing a Tatar sheepskin cap. He waved his hand and all three began lugging something out of the boat that was so heavy that I can't think why the boat hadn't sunk. They all took a bundle on their shoulders and set off along the shore. I soon lost sight of them. I had to get back, but I was very concerned by these weird doings, I don't mind saying, and impatiently waited for morning to come.

When my Cossack woke up he was very surprised to find me fully dressed, but I didn't tell him the reason for it. I spent some time at the window admiring the view. The blue sky was dotted with scattered clouds, the far Crimean shore was a mauve streak on the horizon, ending in a cliff topped by the white tower of a lighthouse. I set out for the fort of Phanagoria to find out from the commandant when I could leave for Gelenjik. But, alas, the commandant couldn't give a definite answer. All the ships at the quay were either coastguard vessels or merchantmen that had still to take on cargo.

'There might be a packet boat in three or four days,' he said. 'We'll see about it then.'

I went back to my lodging, depressed and annoyed, to be met at the door by my Cossack, who looked scared.

'It looks bad, sir,' he said.

'Yes,' I answered. 'Heaven alone knows when we'll get out of here.'

At this he grew even more agitated and, leaning towards me, whispered:

'This place – it's unwholesome. I met up with a Black Sea Cossack I know today, a sergeant – he was in my unit a year back. When I told him where we were, he said the place was unwholesome and the people a bad lot. And he's right, too. What can you make of that blind boy? He goes everywhere on his own, fetches the water, goes down to the market for bread. Everybody here seems to take it for granted.'

'Well, what of it? Has the woman come back?'

'Yes, she came while you were out. She's brought her daughter.'

'Daughter? She hasn't got one.'

'Well, I don't know who it can be if it's not her daughter. Anyway, the old woman's in there in the hut now.'

I went into the hovel. The stove was going full blast and the meal being cooked on it looked rather lavish for poor folk. All my questions to the old woman met with the reply that she was deaf and couldn't hear. There was no point in going on, so I turned to the blind boy, who sat in front of the stove, putting sticks on the fire. I took hold of his ear.

'Now then, you blind imp,' I said. 'Where were you going with that bundle last night, eh?'

The boy suddenly burst into tears, bawling and whining.

'Where to?' he said (once more in Ukrainian). 'I didn't go anywhere. Bundle? What bundle?'

This time the old woman heard.

'Making things up,' she grumbled, 'and blaming it on a poor afflicted boy. What are you getting on to him for? What's he done to you?'

I'd had enough of this and went out, determined to get to the bottom of this mystery.

Pulling my cape around me, I sat down on a stone by the fence and gazed into the distance. Before me lay the sea, still rough after last night's storm, its monotonous din like the murmur of a town as it falls asleep. It reminded me of the old days and took my mind back to our cold northern capital. Stirred by these memories, I sat lost in thought.

An hour had gone by, perhaps more, when I suddenly heard what sounded like a song. Yes, it was a song, sung by the young, clear voice of a woman. But where was it coming from? I listened. It was an odd tune, slow and melancholy, then quick and lively. I looked around, but there was nobody about. I listened again. The sound seemed to come from the sky. I looked up and there, standing on the roof of my hut, was a girl in a striped dress, her hair flowing loose like a mermaid's. She was gazing out to sea, shielding her eyes from the sun with her hand. One moment she laughed, talking to herself, then she would start singing again. I can remember every word of it.

> Tall ships sail o'er the deep green ocean,
> White sails set on the billowy wave.
> My little boat sails there with the tall ships,
> Sails has she none, just her two good oars.

Storm winds will blow, and the old tall ships
Will lift their wings and fly over the sea.
Then I'll curtsey and beg so humbly:
'Have pity on my boat, oh wicked sea.
'Precious are the goods that my boat carries,
'Bold is the heart that steers her through the night.'

I couldn't help thinking that I'd heard this voice the night before. I thought for a moment, and when I next looked at the roof the girl was gone. Suddenly, she darted past me, humming a different tune and snapping her fingers, and ran inside to the old woman. There was an argument; the old woman speaking angrily, the girl laughing loudly. Then again I saw my sprite skipping towards me. She stopped as she reached me and stared me in the eye, as though surprised at my being there, then nonchalantly turned away and walked slowly off towards the quay.

That wasn't the end of it, though, because she hung around my quarters all day, singing and skipping. She was a strange creature. There were no signs of madness in her face – in fact, when she looked at me, her eyes were bright and penetrating. They appeared to have some magnetic power and seemed always to be expecting some question, but as soon as I spoke, she would run off with a crafty smile.

I had never seen a woman like her before. She wasn't at all beautiful, though I have my prejudices on the subject of beauty too. She had plenty of breeding, and breeding in a woman, as in a horse, means a lot – a discovery first made by *la jeune France*. It (breeding, that is, not *la jeune France*) comes out chiefly in a woman's walk, in her hands and feet, the nose being specially significant. In Russia a well-shaped nose is rarer than a tiny foot.

My singer appeared to be no older than eighteen. I was enchanted by the extraordinary suppleness of her figure, the special tilt she gave to her head, the golden tint of her lightly-tanned neck and shoulders, her long auburn hair, and, above all, her well-shaped nose. True, there was something wild and suspicious about her sidelong glances, and an elusive quality in the way she smiled, but such is the power of prejudice that my head was completely turned by her regular nose. I thought I had lighted on Goethe's Mignon, that fabulous product of his German imagination. Indeed, they had much in common – the same sudden changes of mood, from restless activity to complete inertia, the same enigmatic speeches, the same skipping, the same strange songs.

Late in the afternoon I stopped her in the doorway and we had the following conversation.

'Tell me, my pretty one,' I said. 'What were you doing up on the roof today?'

'Looking to see which way the wind blew.'

'And why did you want to know that?'

'Happiness comes the way the wind blows.'

'Was your song meant to bring you happiness then?'

'Happiness goes with a song.'

'And what if your song brings you to grief?'

'What if it does? If things don't get better, they get worse, and it's a short road that leads from bad to good.'

'Who taught you that song?'

'Nobody taught me. I sing whatever comes into my head. It'll be heard by the one it's meant for, and you won't understand if you're not meant to hear.'

'And what's your name, my songstress?'

'Ask the man who christened me.'

'And who was he?'

'How should I know?'

'We are mysterious, aren't we,' I said. 'Well, there's something I do know about you.' There was no change in her expression, not even a flicker of her lips – I might have been talking of someone else. 'I know you went down to the shore last night.'

And I gave her a very solemn account of all that I had seen, expecting to confuse her, but not on your life! She just gave a loud laugh.

'It's plenty you saw, but little you know,' she said. 'And what you do know, you'd better keep to yourself.'

'And supposing, for instance, I decided to report it to the commandant?' I said, looking extremely solemn, even severe.

With a sudden hop, however, she burst into song and vanished like a bird startled from a bush. My final words were inopportune. I had no idea of their importance at the time, but later had occasion to regret them.

As soon as it was dark, I told my Cossack to heat up the teapot camp-style, then lit a candle and sat down at the table, taking an occasional puff at my travelling pipe. I was just finishing my second glass of tea when the door creaked and I heard footsteps and the light rustle of a dress behind me. I gave a start and turned round. It was my mermaid. She quietly sat down opposite me, saying nothing, but gazing at me with a look that seemed wonderfully tender. It reminded me of those looks that had played such havoc with my life in the old days. She appeared to expect some question, but for some reason I was filled with embarrassment and said nothing. You could tell she was excited from the dull pallor of her face, and I noticed a faint tremor in her hand as it strayed aimlessly over the table. One moment her bosom heaved, the next she seemed to be holding her breath. I was beginning to feel I'd had enough of this comedy and was on the point of putting a highly prosaic end to the silence – by offering her a glass of tea – when she suddenly leapt up, threw her arms round my neck and a moist, passionate kiss sounded on my lips. It went black before my eyes, my head swam, and I embraced her with all the force of youthful passion. But, with a whispered command to go to the beach that night when all were asleep, she slid snake-like through my arms and darted from the room. In the hallway she knocked over the teapot and a candle that stood on the floor.

'She-devil!' yelled my Cossack, who had settled down on some straw, intending to warm himself with what was left of the tea. Only then did I come down to earth.

Two hours later, when all was quiet on the quay, I roused my Cossack.

'If I fire my pistol, run down to the beach,' I said.

His eyes bulged, and he replied automatically, 'Very good, sir.' I stuck a pistol in my belt and went out.

She was waiting for me at the edge of the cliff. Her clothing was scant, to say the least, with a light shawl round her supple waist.

'This way,' she said. She took my hand and we began the descent. I still don't know how I escaped breaking my neck. At the bottom we turned to the right and took the path along which I had followed the blind boy the night before. The moon was not yet up, and two solitary stars shone like warning lights in the deep blue sky. The ponderous waves came in with steady rhythmic beat, barely lifting the lone boat that lay moored by the shore.

'Let's get into the boat,' said my companion.

I hesitated. I'm not at all keen on sentimental boat-trips, but this was no time for holding back, so I followed her into the boat, and before I realized what was happening we were afloat.

'What's this all about?' I asked angrily.

'This is what it's about,' she said, pushing me on to the seat and putting her arms around me. 'I love you.'

Her cheek pressed against mine, and I felt her fiery breath upon my face. Suddenly there was a loud splash as something fell into the water. I grabbed for my belt – and found my pistol gone. I suddenly had a horrible suspicion. The blood surged in my head. I looked round – we were a hundred yards from shore and I couldn't swim! I tried to push her away, but she clung to my clothes like a cat, and with a sudden push nearly had me in the sea. The boat rocked, but I steadied myself, and a desperate struggle began. My fury gave me extra strength, but I saw I was no match for my opponent when it came to agility.

'What is it you want?' I cried, squeezing her tiny hands till the bones crunched. But with her serpentlike nature she bore the pain and made no cry.

'You saw,' she said. 'You'll tell on us.'

Then, with a superhuman effort, she hurled me across the gunwale, and we both hung over the side of the boat, with her hair touching the water. It was a critical moment. Bracing my knee against the bottom of the boat, I seized her hair with one hand and her throat with the other. She let go of my clothes, and in an instant I pushed her into the sea. It was quite dark now. I glimpsed her head a couple of times in the spray, and that was all.

I found half an old oar in the bottom of the boat and after much labour somehow reached the quay. As I made my way back to the hut along the shore I automatically looked towards the place where the blind boy had awaited the nocturnal sailor the night before. The moon was up now and I fancied I saw someone in white sitting on the beach. Filled with curiosity, I crept nearer and dropped down in the grass above the cliff. By raising my head slightly I had a good view of all that was going on below and was not very surprised, in fact I was almost glad, to see that it was my mermaid. She was wringing the spray from her long hair, and her wet frock showed the outline of her supple waist and high bosom.

A boat soon appeared in the distance. It came swiftly in to shore and a man got out, as on the previous night. He wore a

Tatar cap, though his head was shaved like a Cossack, and he had a large knife sticking from his belt.

'Yanko,' said the girl. 'Everything's ruined.'

They went on talking, but so quietly that I couldn't make out what they were saying.

'Where's the blind boy?' asked Yanko at last in a louder voice.

'I've sent him for the things,' said the girl.

He appeared a few minutes later carrying a sack on his back, which was stowed in the boat.

'Listen you, blind boy,' said Yanko. 'Keep an eye on the place . . . you know where, don't you. There's valuable stuff there. Tell (I didn't catch the name) that I've finished taking orders from him. Things are going wrong, and this is the last he'll see of me. It's too dangerous. I'll go and look for a job somewhere else. He won't find another daredevil chap like me, and you tell him that I'd never have left him if he'd paid better. But I go where I please, wherever the wind blows and the sea roars.' There was a pause, then Yanko said: 'She's going with me. She can't stay here now. And tell the old woman it's time she died. She's lived too long, she's had her time. She won't see us again.'

'What about me?' asked the blind boy plaintively.

'You're no concern of mine,' said Yanko.

Meanwhile, my mermaid had jumped into the boat and waved to her companion. Yanko put something in the blind boy's hand and said:

'Here, buy yourself some gingerbread.'

'Is that all I get?' asked the blind boy.

'There's another then,' said Yanko, and I heard the ring of a coin falling on the rocks. The blind boy didn't pick it up.

Yanko got into the boat, and hoisting a small sail, they sailed swiftly away before the off-shore wind. For a long time the white sail could be seen in the moonlight, bobbing among the dark waves. The blind boy still sat on the shore, and I heard what sounded like sobbing. He was crying. He cried and cried.

I felt sad. Why did fate toss me into the peaceful midst of these *honest smugglers*? I had shattered their calm, like a stone thrown into a still pool – and like a stone, too, I had nearly gone to the bottom.

I went back to my lodging. The guttering candle flickered on a wooden platter in the hallway. Despite my orders, my Cossack was sleeping like a log, with his gun in his hands. I didn't disturb him, but took the candle and went inside the hut. To my dismay I found my box, silver-mounted sabre and Daghestan dagger (the gift of a friend) had all vanished. Now I knew what that damned boy had been carrying! I roused my Cossack with a none too friendly shove and cursed him angrily. But there was nothing I could do. I could hardly go and complain to the authorities that I'd been robbed by a blind boy and very nearly drowned by a girl of eighteen.

Next morning there was a ship, thank God, and I left Taman. I've no idea what became of the old woman and the poor blind boy. And anyway, the joys and tribulations of mankind are of no concern to me, an itinerant officer with a travel warrant in my pocket.

2

PRINCESS MARY

11 May

I ARRIVED in Pyatigorsk yesterday and took lodgings in the outskirts, high up at the foot of Mashuk. When there's a storm the clouds will come right down to my roof. When I opened my window at five this morning, the room filled with the scent of flowers from the modest garden outside. Branches of cherry blossom peep in at my window and the wind sends occasional showers of white petals on to my desk. I have magnificent views on three sides – to the west lies Beshtau with its five blue peaks, like 'the last cloud of the dying storm'; to the north Mashuk towers like a shaggy Persian cap, filling the whole horizon; to the east the view is gayer – below me, in a splash of colour, lies the little town, all neat and new, with the babbling of medicinal springs and the clamour of the multi-lingual throng. Beyond the town stands a massive amphitheatre of mountains, bluer and hazier in the distance, while along the horizon stretches a silver chain of snowy peaks with Kazbek at one end and the twin summits of Elbrus at the other.

It's a delight to live in a place like this. Every fibre of my body tingles with joy. The air is pure and fresh, as the kiss of a child, the sun is bright, the sky is blue – what more can one want? What need have we here of passions, desires, regrets?

However, enough of that. I'm off to the Elizabeth spring. I hear all the spa society gathers there in the morning.

*

91

I went down to the centre of the town and walked along the boulevard, meeting several pathetic groups going slowly up the hill. They were mostly steppe landowners' families, as you could tell at a glance from the husbands' old-fashioned threadbare coats and the dressy clothes of the wives and daughters. They evidently keep a check on all the spa bachelors, for they studied me with tender interest. They were taken in for a moment by the Petersburg cut of my coat, but when they saw my epaulettes were those of a mere line regiment, they turned away in disgust.

The wives of the local dignitaries – what you might call the ladies of the waters – were better disposed. They carry *lorgnettes* and bother less about a man's uniform, for, living in the Caucasus, they're used to finding ardent hearts and cultured minds under the plain numbered buttons and white cap of a line officer. They are very charming ladies and their charm is not short-lived. They have a new set of admirers each year – perhaps that's the secret of their unfailing amiability.

As I climbed the narrow path to the Elizabeth spring, I passed a good number of men, some civilians, some soldiers, who, I later found out, form a special class among those awaiting the movement of the waters. They drink (though not the waters), rarely take walks, and are only half-heartedly interested in women. They spend their time gambling and complaining that they're bored. They are dandies, too, and strike classic poses as they lower their wicker-cased tumblers into the sulphur spring. The civilians sport pale blue cravats, and the military types have ruffs showing above their collars. They admit to a profound scorn for all provincial houses and sigh for the aristocratic salons of the capital (where they are not received).

At last I came to the well. Just by it, on the little square, they have put up a red-roofed building to house the baths, and a short distance away there is a covered terrace where people can promenade when it rains. Some wounded officers were sitting on a bench, looking pale and sad, their crutches drawn in to their feet. A few ladies were walking briskly up and down the square, waiting for the waters to take effect. There were two or three pretty faces among them, and in the vine walks on the slopes of Mashuk I caught an occasional glimpse of the gaily-coloured bonnets of ladies fond of solitude *à deux* – for I saw that each bonnet was accompanied by a military cap or a monstrous round hat. Silhouetted on the steep cliff, where the pavilion called 'The Harp of Aeolus' stands, were sightseers aiming their telescopes at Elbrus. Among them were two tutors and their charges, here to take the cure for scrofula.

I stopped, out of breath, at the edge of the cliff and leaned against the corner of the baths to look at the beautiful view all round. Suddenly I heard a familiar voice behind me.

'Why, Pechorin! Have you been here long?'

I turned round. It was Grushnitsky. We embraced. I'd first met him at the front. He'd been wounded in the leg and had come to the spa the week before me.

Grushnitsky is a cadet. He's only been in the army a year and out of some peculiar brand of dandyism goes around in a thick private's greatcoat. He's got the St George's Cross. He is well built, with dark complexion and black hair. To look at him you might take him for twenty-five, though in fact he is barely twenty-one. When he talks, he has a habit of tossing his head back, and all the time he twirls his moustache with his left hand, and holds his crutch with the right. He speaks quickly, affectedly, and is one of those people who have a fine sentiment ready for every occasion in life, but lack all sense of beauty and make a solemn display of uncommon emotions, exalted passions and exceptional sufferings. Their greatest pleasure in life is to create an effect, and romantic provincial ladies find them madly attractive. When they get older, they settle down as country squires or take to drink, or occasionally both. They often have many good qualities, but they never have a scrap of poetry in them.

Grushnitsky has a special passion for declamation. The moment the conversation goes beyond ordinary topics he bombards you with words. I could never argue with him, for he never answers your objections or even listens to you. As soon as you stop speaking, he launches into a long tirade, supposedly bearing on what you said, but in fact merely continuing his speech.

He is quite witty, and his epigrams are often amusing, though never pointed or savage – he'll never slay anyone with a word. He knows nothing of people or of the weaker sides of human nature, since the sole preoccupation of his life has been himself. His ambition is to become the hero of a novel. He's spent so much time trying to convince others that he's not of this world and that fate has some mysterious trials in store for him, that he practically believes it himself. That's why he flaunts the thick private's greatcoat.

I've seen through him, and that's why he dislikes me – though to all appearances we are on the best of terms. He is reputed to be very brave, but I've seen him in action: he waves his sword and charges forward shouting, eyes half-closed. Not exactly the Russian type of bravery.

I don't like him either. I fancy one day our paths will cross and one of us will come off worst.

His being in the Caucasus is also due to his mania for romantic situations. I'm sure that he spent his last evening at home gloomily explaining to some pretty neighbour that he wasn't going just in the normal course of duty, but was going in search of death, because. . . . At this point he probably hid his eyes and said 'No, you mustn't know the reason. The shock would be too great for your pure heart. Anyway, what point would there be? What am I to you? Will you ever understand me?' – and so on.

He told me himself that his reason for joining the K— regiment would always remain a secret between himself and the Almighty.

Still, when he drops the tragic line Grushnitsky is quite agreeable and entertaining. I'm curious to see him with women. I imagine he really puts it on then.

We met like old friends. I asked him about spa life and people of interest. He sighed.

'It's a pretty dull life we lead here,' he said. 'The people who drink water in the morning are lifeless like all invalids, and the ones who drink wine in the evening are insufferable like all healthy people. There's some female society – but that's small comfort. They play whist, dress badly and their French is terrible. There's only Princess Ligovskoy from Moscow this year. She's here with her daughter, but I'm not acquainted with them. My private's greatcoat stamps me as an outcast. I find it hard to take the sympathy it brings me – it's like charity.'

Just then two ladies walked past us towards the well, one elderly, the other young, with a good figure. I couldn't see the faces beneath their hats, but they were dressed in the strictest good taste – nothing excessive. The young one wore a high-necked pearl-grey dress, with a light silk scarf round her supple neck. Her dark brown boots fitted so trimly round her slender ankles that even a person uninitiated in the mysteries of beauty would have certainly gasped, if only with surprise. In her light, yet dignified walk there was a virginal quality too elusive to define, but obvious when seen. As she passed us, there was a breath of that indescribable fragrance that sometimes wafts from the letter of a woman one loves.

'That's Princess Ligovskoy,' said Grushnitsky. 'And that's

her daughter. She calls her Mary, in the English fashion. They've only been here three days.'

'Yet you know her Christian name already?'

Grushnitsky blushed.

'I happened to hear it,' he said. 'I must say I've no wish to make their acquaintance. These proud aristocrats think soldiers like us uncouth, just because we're not in the Guards. Little they care what intellect or feeling there might be beneath an infantry cap and a thick greatcoat.'

I smiled.

'Your poor greatcoat!' I said. 'And who's the man going up and giving them their glasses with such attention?'

'Oh, that's Rayevich, some dandy from Moscow. He's a gambler too – you can tell by the blue waistcoat and that enormous gold chain looped across it. Look how thick his stick is – it would do for Robinson Crusoe. So would the beard, for that matter, and his peasant's haircut.'

'You've got a down on the whole human race,' I said.

'I've good reason to.'

'Oh, really?'

At this point the ladies moved away from the well and came level with us. With the aid of his crutch Grushnitsky struck a dramatic pose and answered me loudly in French:

'*Mon cher, je haïs les hommes pour ne pas les mépriser, car autrement la vie serait une farce trop dégoutante.*'

The pretty young princess turned and bestowed a long, curious look on the speech-maker. The feeling conveyed in her look was very hard to define, but it wasn't scorn – on which I felt Grushnitsky was to be warmly congratulated.

'This Princess Mary is very pretty,' I said. 'She's got such velvet eyes. "Velvet" is just the right word – I suggest you borrow it when you talk about her eyes. The top and bottom lashes are so long that the pupils don't reflect the sunlight. I like eyes that don't shine. They're so soft, they seem to stroke you. Actually, her whole face seems excellent. Are her teeth white? That's very important. Pity she didn't smile at that fine phrase of yours.'

'You talk about a pretty woman as if she were an English thoroughbred,' declared Grushnitsky indignantly.

'*Mon cher*,' I replied, trying to capture his tone. '*Je méprise les femmes pour ne pas les aimer, car autrement la vie serait un mélodrame trop ridicule.*'

I turned and walked away. I spent half an hour strolling about the vine walks and limestone cliffs and the bushes on the slopes between. It was growing hot, so I hurried to get home.

As I passed the sulphur spring, I stopped to get my breath in the shade of the covered terrace and chanced to see a somewhat curious scene. The actors were placed as follows: the old princess and the Moscow dandy sat on a bench in the covered terrace, apparently deep in earnest talk; the young princess, having presumably finished her last glass of water, was walking pensively up and down by the well, at the side of which Grushnitsky was standing. There was no one else about.

I went closer and hid round the corner of the terrace. Just then Grushnitsky dropped his glass on the gravel and struggled to bend and pick it up, but was hampered by his wounded leg. Poor fellow, how hard he tried, leaning on his crutch, but all in vain. There was a look of quite genuine suffering on his soulful face. Princess Mary saw all this better than I did, and, light as a bird, she tripped forward, stooped, picked up the glass and gave it to him with a gesture of indescribable charm. Then she blushed deeply and looked back at the terrace, but once she had made sure that Mama had seen nothing, she immediately regained her composure. By the time Grushnitsky opened his mouth to thank her she was gone.

A minute later she came out of the terrace with her mother

and Rayevich, but as she passed Grushnitsky she put on a look of solemn decorum and never turned or noticed the long passionate look with which he followed her down the hill till she disappeared among the lime-trees on the boulevard. There was a glimpse of her hat across the street as she went through the gate of one of the best houses in Pyatigorsk. The old princess followed after taking leave of Rayevich at the gate.

Only then did poor smitten Grushnitsky notice I was there.

'Did you see?' he said, shaking me firmly by the hand. 'She's an absolute angel.'

'Why?' I asked, looking all innocent.

'Do you mean you didn't see?'

'Certainly I saw. She picked up your glass. An attendant would have done the same if he'd been here, and a good deal quicker too, in hopes of a tip. Though it's easy enough to see why she felt sorry for you, after the terrible face you pulled when you put your weight on your bad leg.'

'And weren't you the least bit moved to see the way her face lit up?'

'No, I wasn't.'

I lied, but I wanted to bait him. I was born with a passion for contradiction. My whole life has been nothing but a series of dismal, unsuccessful attempts to go against heart or reason. An enthusiast turns me cold as ice, and I fancy that frequent contact with an apathetic idler would turn me into an ardent idealist. I admit, too, that at this moment I felt a twinge of something else, unpleasant, though familiar – envy. I say 'envy' straight out, for I'm accustomed to be frank with myself. And I doubt whether any young man, who has lived in society and grown used to indulging his vanity, can avoid a pang of jealousy when he sees a pretty woman who's taken his idle fancy favour another, whom she knows no better than himself.

Grushnitsky and I went down the hill in silence, then walked along the boulevard. We passed the windows of the house into which our belle had vanished. She was sitting at the window. Grushnitsky tugged my sleeve and gave her one of those languorous looks that have so little effect on women. I eyed her with my *lorgnette* and saw that she smiled at Grushnitsky's look, but was genuinely angered by my presumption. And, indeed, how dare a Caucasian line officer turn his *lorgnette* on a Moscow princess!

13 May

This morning the doctor called. His name is Werner, though he's a Russian. There's nothing so odd about that – I once knew a man called Ivanov who was a German.

Werner is a remarkable man in many ways. Like most doctors, he's a sceptic and a materialist, but he's also a poet of the true sort – always a poet in what he does and often, too, in what he says, though he's never written a line of verse in his life. He's studied all the living chords of the human heart in the way other people might study the sinews of a dead body. He's never managed to apply his knowledge, though, just as a first-rate anatomist sometimes has no idea how to cure a fever. As a rule Werner laughs at his patients behind their backs, but I once saw him in tears over a dying soldier. Werner was poor and dreamed of millions, but he would never lift a finger for the sake of money. He once told me he would rather do a favour to an enemy than a friend. The latter would mean selling his charity, while his enemy would hate him the more for his generosity.

He has a wicked tongue, and his epigrams have caused more than one honest fellow to be written off as an idiot. His rivals, the jealous spa doctors, spread a rumour that he did caricatures of his patients. The patients were furious and most of them would have nothing more to do with him. His friends – every truly honest man serving in the Caucasus, that is – tried to restore his fallen stock, but failed.

He has one of those faces that seem disagreeable at first sight, but become attractive later, when one comes to recognize in its irregular features the mark of a tried and noble spirit. There have been cases of women falling madly in love with such people, preferring their ugliness to the beauty of the freshest, rosiest-cheeked Endymions. Give women their due – they have an instinctive sense of inner beauty. Perhaps that is why men like Werner are so passionately fond of them.

Werner is short, thin and as weak as a child. He has one leg shorter than the other, like Byron, and his head looks disproportionately large for his body. His hair is close cropped, and shows up the bumps of his skull, which would astonish a phrenologist by their strange mixture of opposing tendencies. His small black eyes are never still, always probing your thoughts. His dress is tasteful and neat, with his small, slender, sinewy hands resplendent in pale yellow gloves. His coat, cravat and waistcoat were invariably black. The young men always called him Mephistopheles, and he pretended to be annoyed, though in fact it flattered his vanity.

We soon understood each other and became close acquaintances, for I'm incapable of friendship. Of two friends one is always the slave of the other, though often neither will admit it. I can never be a slave, and to command in these circumstances is too exacting, for you have to pretend at the same time. Besides, I have money and servants enough.

Our association began when I met Werner in S— at a noisy, crowded party of young men. As the evening wore on, the conversation turned to matters philosophical and metaphysical. They were discussing beliefs, and everyone believed in something or other.

'For my part,' said Werner, 'I'm convinced of only one thing.'

'What's that?' I asked, anxious to hear his views, for so far he had said nothing.

'That one fine day, sooner or later, I shall die,' he answered.

'I'm better off than you,' I said. 'I'm convinced of another thing too – that one foul evening I had the misfortune to be born.'

They all thought we were talking nonsense, though in fact no one had said anything more sensible than this the whole evening. From then on we marked each other out in the crowd, came together a number of times and discoursed very solemnly on abstract subjects until we saw that each of us was pulling the other's leg. Then we looked each other meaningly in the eye, as Cicero says the Roman augurs did, and burst out laughing. We had a good laugh and separated, well pleased with our evening.

I was lying on the couch, gazing at the ceiling with my hands under my head, when Werner came into the room. He stood his cane in the corner, sat down, yawned and announced that it was getting hot outside. I said that I found the flies troublesome, and we lapsed into silence.

'My dear Doctor,' I said. 'What a dull place the world would be if there were no fools. Here we are, two intelligent men, who know you can argue eternally about everything under the sun, so we don't argue. We each know practically all the other's innermost thoughts. With us a single word speaks volumes. We see through the triple outer husk to the kernel of our emotions. We find sad things funny and funny things sad, though in fact we're pretty indifferent to everything except ourselves. So there can be no exchange of feelings or ideas between us – we each know all we want to know about the other and have no wish to know more. All we can do is tell each other news. Have you got any to tell me?'

I closed my eyes and yawned, exhausted by this long speech.

Werner pondered a moment, then said:

'All that rigmarole of yours has got some purpose.'

'It's got two,' I replied.

'You tell me one, and I'll tell you the other,' he said.

'All right. You begin,' I said, still studying the ceiling, and smiling to myself.

'You'd like some information about a certain person who's arrived here. I can guess who it is you're interested in, because there have already been inquiries about you in that quarter.'

'Upon my word, Doctor, it's impossible for us to talk together. We read each other's minds.'

'And what's the other purpose?' he said.

'The other purpose was to make you talk – because firstly, listening is less exhausting than talking; secondly, there's no danger of saying more than you mean to; thirdly, there's the chance you might find out another's secret; and fourthly, an intelligent man like you prefers people who listen to people who talk. Now, to business. What did the old princess say about me?'

'You're quite sure it was the old princess and not the young one?'

'Absolutely.'

'Why?'

'Because the young princess asked about Grushnitsky.'

'You've a great gift of understanding,' said Werner. 'She told me she was sure the young man in the private's greatcoat had been reduced to the ranks because of a duel.'

'I trust you didn't destroy that pleasant illusion?'

'Naturally.'

'The stage is set,' I cried, delighted. 'We'll see if we can provide a *dénouement* for this comedy. Evidently fate means to see I'm not bored.'

'I fancy poor Grushnitsky's going to be your victim.'

'What else happened, Doctor?'

'The old princess said your face seemed familiar. I said she must have met you in Petersburg. She knew your name when I mentioned it. Your affair seems to have caused quite a stir. The princess talked about your escapades – society gossip with something of her own thrown in, I dare say. The daughter was very interested and evidently saw you as the hero of some novel in the modern taste. I didn't argue with the princess, though I knew she was talking nonsense.'

'You're a friend indeed,' I said and held out my hand. Werner shook it warmly.

'I'll introduce you if you like,' he said.

'Really, Doctor,' I said, throwing up my hands in horror. 'Heroes are never introduced. There's only one way for them to meet the girl, and that's to save her from certain death.'

'Are you really going to court the young princess then?'

'No, no, quite the contrary. I triumph at last, Doctor – you fail to understand me.' I paused for a moment. 'And yet I'm sorry you do,' I went on. 'I never give away my secrets. I like people to guess them, then I can always reject them when it suits me. However, you must give me a description of the mother and daughter. What are they like?'

'The mother, for a start, is a woman of forty-five. She's got a splendid digestion, but there's something wrong with her blood – she's got red patches on her cheeks. She's spent the latter half of her life in Moscow and has put on weight with the quiet life she's led there. She's fond of spicy stories and isn't too careful what she says herself when the daughter's not there. She told me her daughter's as pure as a dove. What do I care? I felt like telling her not to worry, as I wouldn't pass it on. The mother's taking the cure for rheumatism, and the daughter for God knows what. I told them both to take two glasses of sulphur water a day and chemical baths twice a week. The old princess doesn't seem used to giving orders, and has got a great respect for her daughter's intelligence and learning because she's read Byron in English and knows algebra. The girls in Moscow seem to have gone academic. Good for them! The men are such boors anyway that flirting with them must be more than any intelligent woman can stand. The old princess likes young people, but the daughter rather looks down on them. She's picked that up in Moscow, where middle-aged wits are the staple fare.'

'Have you ever been in Moscow?'

'Yes, I had something of a practice there once.'

'Do go on.'

'I think I've told you everything. Oh no, there's one more thing. The young princess seems to like talking about emotions, passions and that sort of thing. She's had one winter in Petersburg and didn't like it, especially the social life. She probably had a cool reception.'

'You saw no one at their house today?'

'Yes, I did. There was an adjutant, an affected Guards officer and a lady, newly arrived here. She's related to the princess by marriage. Very pretty, but very ill by the look of things. You may have met her at the well? Average height, fair hair, regular features, looks consumptive from the colour of her face. She's got a dark mole on her right cheek. I was struck by her – she's got a very expressive face.'

'A mole,' I muttered. 'Is it possible?'

Werner looked at me, put his hand on my heart and declared triumphantly:

'You know her!'

It was true, my heart was beating faster than normal.

'It's your turn to crow,' I said. 'But I trust you won't give me away. Though I've not yet seen her, I'm sure from your description that it's an old flame of mine. Don't say a word to her about me. If she asks, say something bad about me.'

'As you please,' said Werner, with a shrug.

When he'd gone, I felt a desperate pang of sadness. Here in the Caucasus our paths had crossed once more. Or had she come on purpose, knowing she would meet me? How would we meet? And, anyway, was it her? My premonitions have never deceived me. There's no one so susceptible to the power of the past as I am. Every memory of past joy or sorrow stabs at my heart and strikes the same old chords. It's silly the way I'm made: I forget nothing – absolutely nothing.

After dinner, at about six o'clock, I walked along the boulevard. There were a lot of people. Princess Ligovskoy and her daughter were sitting on a bench, surrounded by young men all doing their utmost to make themselves agreeable. I positioned myself on another bench some distance away and stopped two officers I knew from the D— regiment. I began spinning some tale, and it must have been very funny, for they roared with laughter. Some of the princess's entourage came over to see what was up, and gradually they all drifted away to join my group. I kept on talking. My stories were clever to the point of stupidity, my comments on the oddities of the passers-by biting to the point of fury. I kept my audience amused till sunset. Princess Mary walked past several times on her mother's arm, escorted by an old fellow with a limp, and several times, as her eye fell on me, she looked annoyed, despite her efforts to appear indifferent.

'What was he telling you?' she asked one young man who, out of politeness, had gone back to her. 'It must have been most interesting. Perhaps it was about his exploits in battle?'

She said this quite loudly, most likely intending to pique me.

'Aha!' I thought. 'You're really angry, my dear Princess. Just wait. There's more to come.'

Grushnitsky followed her around like some predatory animal, never taking his eyes off her. I bet tomorrow he'll be asking for someone to introduce him to the mother. She's bored, so she'll be very pleased.

16 May

My affairs have come on tremendously these last two days. Princess Mary positively hates me. I've already heard two or three epigrams she has made up about me, quite pointed, but very flattering all the same. She just can't understand why I, who am used to good society and on such close terms with her Petersburg cousins and aunts, don't attempt to make her acquaintance. We meet every day at the well or on the boulevard, and I try my best to draw away her admirers – the glittering adjutants, the pale Muscovites, and so on – and I almost always succeed. I've always hated entertaining, but now every day my house is full of guests, dining, supping, gambling. It's a sad fact, but my champagne is more than a match for her magnetic eyes.

I met her in Chelakhov's shop yesterday. She was haggling over the price of a Persian rug and pleading with Mama not to begrudge her it, as it would look so nice in her study. I offered forty roubles more and bought it from under her nose. I was rewarded with a superb look of fury. Near dinner time I had my horse walked specially past her windows with the rug draped over him. Werner was visiting them at the time and told me that the effect of this scene was most dramatic. Princess Mary wants to launch a crusade against me, and I've noticed that two of the adjutants bow very stiffly to me when they are with her – but every day they dine at my table.

Grushnitsky has put on a militant air. He goes around with his hands behind his back, recognizing no one. His leg has suddenly got better, and he hardly limps at all. He's found some opportunity of talking to Princess Ligovskoy and paying some compliment to Princess Mary. She can't be very discriminating, for since then she's been giving him the sweetest smile when he bows to her.

'Are you quite sure you don't want to meet the Ligovskoys?' he asked me yesterday.

'Quite sure,' I said.

'But really! It's the most agreeable house in the place. All the best people . . .'

'My dear fellow, I've had enough of society anywhere, let alone this place. Do you visit them then?'

'Not as yet. I've talked a couple of times with the daughter, that's all. But it's rather embarrassing angling for an invitation, even if it is the done thing here. It'd be a different matter if I were commissioned.'

'Oh, come now. You're far more interesting as you are. You just don't know how to make the most of your advantages. Why, with that private's greatcoat, every sentimental girl takes you for a hero, a martyr.'

Grushnitsky smiled conceitedly.

'Nonsense,' he said.

'I'm sure the daughter is in love with you already,' I went on. He blushed violently and puffed himself up.

Oh, vanity! You are the lever with which Archimedes wanted to lift the world.

'You're always joking,' he said, pretending to be angry. 'In the first place, she scarcely knows me as yet.'

'Women only love men they don't know.'

'Naturally, I'm not in the least concerned that she should like me. All I want is to make the acquaintance of a pleasant family. It would be absurd for me to have any hopes . . . Now, with you, for example, it's another matter. A single look from one of you Petersburg lady-killers and women melt. Do you know what Princess Mary said about you?'

'What, she's been talking to you about me already?'

'It's nothing to be pleased about, I'm afraid. I happened to get into conversation with her at the well and practically the first thing she said was "Who is that disagreeable, sombre-looking man? He was with you the other day, when . . ." And she blushed. She wouldn't say which day, when she remembered the charming thing she had done. I told her there was no need to mention the day as it would live in my memory for ever. Pechorin, my friend, I'm afraid you're in her bad books. It's such a pity, for Mary is awfully sweet.'

I should point out that Grushnitsky is one of those men who refer to any woman they scarcely know as 'my Mary', 'my Sophie', if she has the good fortune to appeal to him.

I looked serious, then said:

'Yes, she's not bad looking. But take care, Grushnitsky. Most Russian girls usually only go in for Platonic attachments and never think of marriage. And Platonic love is the most trouble-some sort. The princess, I fancy, is one of those women who want to be amused, and two dull minutes with you will finish you for good. Your silence must rouse her curiosity, your con-versation must leave her wanting more. You've got to play on her feelings all the time. She'll scorn public opinion a dozen times for your sake and call it a sacrifice, but she'll get her own back by giving you hell, and then calmly declare that she can't stand you. If you don't get the upper hand, her first kiss won't give you the right to expect a second. She'll play with you till she's tired of it, then a couple of years later she'll marry some brute out of duty to Mama and persuade herself she's unhappy, because it was not heaven's will to unite her with the only man she ever loved (you, that is) on account of his private's greatcoat, though under that thick grey coat there beat an ardent, noble heart . . .'

Grushnitsky banged his fist on the table and began pacing the room.

I laughed to myself, and even smiled a couple of times, though luckily he didn't see me. He's more confiding than ever, so he must be in love. He's even come out with a silver niello ring made by a local craftsman. I thought it looked fishy, so I examined it, and what did I find? It's got the name 'Mary' engraved in small letters on the inside, with the date when she picked up the celebrated glass. I kept my discovery to myself. I don't want to force confessions from him, I want him to pick me as his confidant – then I'll have fun!

*

I got up late today, and when I got to the well, there was no one there. It was getting hot. Small fluffy white clouds were racing in from the snowy mountains, giving promise of a storm. The summit of Mashuk smoked like an extinguished torch, and wisps of grey cloud coiled and slid round it like snakes, as though entangled and held back by the thorny scrub. The air was vibrant with electricity.

I went into the vine walk that leads to the grotto. I felt sad, thinking of the young woman with the mole on her cheek that Werner had told me about. Why was she here? And was it her? And why did I think it was her? Why was I even sure of it? There are plenty of women with moles on their cheeks.

It was with these thoughts going through my mind that I came to the grotto. A woman was sitting on a stone seat in the cool shade of its vault. She wore a straw hat and was wrapped in a black shawl. Her head was sunk on her breast, her face hidden by her hat. Not wishing to disturb her meditation, I was about to turn back, when she glanced up at me.

'Vera!' I cried involuntarily.

She gave a start and turned pale.

'I knew you were here,' she said.

I sat beside her and took her hand. A long-forgotten thrill passed through my body at the sound of that sweet voice. Her deep, tranquil eyes looked straight into mine, and there was mistrust and something like reproach in them.

'It's been a long time,' I said.

'Yes, it's been a long time. We've both changed a lot.'

'You no longer love me, then?' I said.

'I'm married,' she said.

'Again? But it was the same a few years back, and then it didn't . . .'

She snatched her hand from mine, her cheeks blazing.

'Perhaps you love your second husband?'

She made no reply and turned away.

'Or is he very jealous?'

Silence.

'What then? He must be young, handsome, very rich (that's certain), and you're afraid . . .'

I looked at her and was alarmed by the look of utter despair on her face and the tears gleaming in her eyes.

At last she said in a whisper:

'Tell me, does it amuse you very much to torture me? I ought to hate you. Ever since I've known you, you've brought me nothing but suffering . . .'

Her voice trembled, she leaned towards me and lowered her head upon my breast.

Perhaps that's why you loved me, I thought. Moments of happiness one forgets, but sorrow never.

I clasped her tight in my arms, and so we stayed for a long

time, till in the end our lips came close and met in a thrilling, passionate kiss. Her hands were like ice, her head was burning. And then we had one of those conversations which make no sense on paper, which you can't repeat and can't even remember. The sounds mean more than the words, like in an Italian opera.

She is most anxious I shouldn't meet her husband. He is the old fellow with the limp I saw on the boulevard. She married him for the sake of her son. He's rich and suffers from rheumatism. I didn't allow myself a single gibe at his expense, for she respects him like a father – and will deceive him like a husband. The human heart is a funny thing, particularly the heart of a woman.

Vera's husband, Sergei Vasilievich G—v, is distantly related to Princess Ligovskoy. They live next door to her, and Vera often visits them. I promised Vera I would get an introduction to the Ligovskoys and show an interest in the daughter so as to divert attention from her. This doesn't in the least interfere with my plans. I shall enjoy myself.

Enjoy myself! I've passed that stage in life when all one seeks is happiness and when the heart feels the need to love someone with passion and intensity. Now all I want is to be loved, and by very few people at that. I think I'd even be content with just one lasting attachment – such is the heart's pathetic way.

It's always puzzled me that I've never been a slave to the women I've loved. In fact, I've always mastered them, heart and soul, without even trying. Why is it? Is it because I never care deeply for anything, while they have gone in constant fear of losing me? Or is it the magnetic attraction of a strong personality? Or have I simply never met a woman of real spirit?

I must confess I don't really like strong-willed women. That's not their role in life!

Actually, I do recall one occasion when I loved a woman with a will too strong for me to master. We parted enemies, though perhaps if I'd met her five years later we would have parted differently.

Vera is ill, very ill, though she won't admit it. I'm afraid it might be consumption or what they call *fièvre lente*, a foreign ailment that has no name in Russian.

The storm broke while we were in the grotto and delayed us half an hour. She never asked me to swear to be true or to say if I'd loved other women since we had parted. She trusts me now as unthinkingly as before, and I won't deceive her. She is the one woman in the world I could never deceive. I know we shall soon part again, perhaps this time for ever. We shall each take our own road to the grave, but her memory will always be sacred in my heart. I've told her this and she believes me, though she says she doesn't.

At last we parted. I watched her go, till I lost sight of her hat among the rocks and shrubs. I felt a pang in my heart, as I did at our first parting. How I rejoiced to feel it. Was it youth coming back to me with all its healthy passions, or was it just youth's farewell glance, a parting gift to remember it by? It's absurd when you think that I'm still just a boy to look at. My face is fresh for all its paleness; my limbs are slim and supple; my hair is thick and curly; there's light in my eyes and fire in my blood.

When I reached home, I got on my horse and galloped out into the steppe. I love galloping through long grass on a fiery horse, with the desert wind in my face. I gulp the scented air and peer into the blue distance, trying to make out the hazy shapes that show up more distinctly every minute. Whatever sorrow weighs on the heart, whatever anxiety troubles the mind, it vanishes in a moment. You feel peace at heart, and the troubled mind is cleared by bodily fatigue. There's no woman whose eyes I wouldn't forget when I see the blue sky and the wooded mountains, lit by the southern sun, or hear the roar of a cascading torrent.

I fancy the Cossacks gazing idly from their watch-towers must have puzzled long over the sight of me galloping without cause or purpose, for from my clothes they must have taken me for a Circassian. Actually, I've been told that on horseback and in Circassian dress I look more like a Kabardian than many Kabardians themselves. Indeed, when it comes to this noble warrior's dress, I'm quite a dandy: just the right amount of braid, expensive weapons with a plain finish, the fur on my cap neither too long nor too short, close-fitting leggings and boots, a white *beshmet* and a dark maroon top-coat. I've made a long study of how the hillmen sit a horse, and nothing flatters my vanity more than to be admired for my mastery of the Caucasian riding style. I keep four horses, one for myself and three for my friends, to avoid the tedium of trailing round the countryside all on my own. They're pleased to take my horses, but never ride with me.

It was not till six o'clock that I remembered it was time for dinner. My horse was dead-beat. I came out on the road that leads from Pyatigorsk to the German colony, where people from the spa often go on party excursions. With massive blue mountains all round – Beshtau, Zmeinaya, Zheleznaya, Lysaya – the road winds through patches of scrub and drops into small ravines where roaring streams flow in the shade of tall grass.

In one of these ravines (called locally *balki*) I stopped to water my horse. Just then a glittering, noisy cavalcade came into view along the road, ladies in black or blue riding habits, their escorts in an incongruous mixture of Circassian and Russian costume. At the head rode Grushnitsky and Princess Mary.

Ladies at the spa still believe that the Circassians attack people in broad daylight, and probably because of this Grushnitsky had slung a sabre and a pair of pistols over his private's greatcoat. He looked quite absurd in this heroic attire.

I was hidden by a tall bush, but had a good view of everything through the foliage, and could tell from their faces that they were having a sentimental conversation. They came to the slope, and Grushnitsky took Princess Mary's horse by the bridle. I heard the tail-end of their conversation.

'And are you going to spend the rest of your life in the Caucasus?' asked the princess.

'What is Russia to me?' replied Grushnitsky. 'A country where thousands will scorn me because they are richer than I am, while here my thick greatcoat has not stood in the way of my meeting you.'

The princess blushed.

'Quite the reverse,' she said.

Grushnitsky looked pleased and went on:

'My life will pass stormily, swiftly and unnoticed among the bullets of savage tribesmen, and if each year God grants me one woman's glance as radiant as . . .'

At this point they drew level with me, and, whipping my horse, I rode out from behind the bush.

'*Mon dieu, un circassien!*' cried the princess in horror.

To reassure her completely, I made a slight bow and replied in French:

'*Ne craignez rien, madame. Je ne suis pas plus dangereux que votre cavalier.*'

She was covered with confusion. Was it because of her mistake? Or was it because she thought my reply insolent? I'd rather the latter were correct. Grushnitsky gave me a look of displeasure.

Late in the evening, about eleven, I went for a stroll through the lime walk on the boulevard. The town was asleep, and only in a few windows were there lights. On three sides there were black mountain ridges, offshoots of Mashuk, on whose summit a small, ominous cloud rested. The moon was rising in the east, and in the distance there gleamed a silver fringe of snow-capped mountains. The cries of the sentries merged with the roar of the hot springs which are left to run freely during the night. Occasionally a clatter of hoofs rang along the street, accompanied by the creak of a cart and a doleful Tatar song.

I sat on a bench and pondered. I felt the need to talk to some friend, to pour out my thoughts to somebody. But to whom could I do that? I wondered what Vera was doing at that moment. I'd have given a lot to press her hand just then.

Suddenly I heard footsteps, quick and uneven. It sounded like Grushnitsky, and so it was. I asked him where he had been.

'At Princess Ligovskoy's,' he answered very grandly. 'How well Mary sings!'

'Do you know what?' I said. 'I bet she's no idea you're a cadet and thinks you're an officer who's been reduced to the ranks.'

'She might. What do I care?' he replied absently.

'I just mentioned it,' I said.

'You know, she's furious with you about today. She thought it was a terrible cheek, and I had a job to convince her that you couldn't have meant to offend her, being so well educated and knowing society as you do. She says you look insolent and must think very highly of yourself.'

'She's perfectly right. Aren't you going to take her part then?'

'I'm afraid I haven't the right as yet.'

Aha! I thought, you've got hopes then!

'But it's worse for you,' said Grushnitsky. 'You won't find it easy to get an introduction now. Such a pity. It's quite one of the most agreeable houses I know.'

I smiled to myself.

'The most agreeable house for me at the moment is my own,' I said, yawning, and got up to go.

'Why not admit you're sorry, though?' said Grushnitsky.

'Nonsense! If I feel like it, I'll call on the princess tomorrow evening.'

'We'll see about that!'

'I'll even make advances to Princess Mary if you'd like me to.'

'Oh, yes! – supposing she'll speak to you.'

'I'll just wait till she's fed up with listening to you. Good night.'

'I'm going for a stroll,' said Grushnitsky. 'I just couldn't sleep at the moment. I know – let's go to the restaurant. There'll be gambling, and tonight I must have strong sensations.'

'I hope you lose,' I said, and went home.

21 May

Nearly a week has gone by and I still haven't met the Ligovskoys. I'm waiting for an opening. Grushnitsky follows Princess Mary everywhere like a shadow, and they have endless talks. When will she tire of him? Her mother takes no notice of them, since Grushnitsky is 'not eligible'. Such is the logic of mothers! I've noticed two or three tender looks being exchanged – I must put an end to it.

Yesterday Vera was at the well for the first time. She hasn't been out since we met in the grotto. We lowered our glasses into the well together and, as she leaned over, she whispered:

'Aren't you going to get an introduction to the Ligovskoys then? It's the only place we can meet.'

A reproach. How tedious! Still, I'd earned it.

Incidentally – tomorrow there's a subscription ball in the restaurant saloon, and I'm going to dance the mazurka with Princess Mary.

22 May

The restaurant saloon turned into the Assembly Rooms. By nine o'clock everyone was there, the princess and her daughter among the last to arrive. Many ladies eyed her with envy and malice, because Princess Mary knows how to dress. Those who consider themselves the local aristocracy hid their envy and attached themselves to her. What can you do? In any female society you always get an upper and a lower circle.

Grushnitsky stood in the crowd outside the window, pressing his face to the glass and never taking his eyes off his goddess. She gave him the slightest nod as she passed, and he beamed all over his face.

The dancing began with a *polonaise*, then a waltz was struck up and spurs jingled, coat-tails flew and whirled.

I stood behind a fat lady canopied with pink feathers. The splendour of her dress recalled the age of farthingales, and her coarse blotchy skin the happy days of the beauty spot. The biggest wart on her neck was concealed by a clasp. She was talking to her partner, a captain of dragoons.

'That young Princess Ligovskoy is quite insufferable,' she said. 'Think of it – she bumped against me and never even apologized, and then turned round and quizzed me with her glass. *C'est impayable!* Why should she be so high and mighty? She needs to be taught a lesson.'

'That shouldn't be difficult,' replied the obliging captain, and he went into the next room.

I at once went up to Princess Mary and asked if she would waltz, taking advantage of the free and easy ways of the place which allow you to dance with ladies you don't know.

She could scarcely suppress a smile of triumph, but soon managed to assume an air of complete indifference, or even severity. She casually rested her hand on my shoulder, gave a slight tilt to her head, and we took the floor. I've never known a waist more sensuous or supple. The freshness of her breath was on my face, and occasionally a lock of her hair detached itself in the whirl of the dance and brushed against my burning cheek.

We did three turns (she waltzes amazingly well), at the end of which she was panting, with misted eyes and half-open lips that could barely murmur the obligatory 'Merci, monsieur'.

For a few minutes neither of us spoke. Then, looking very humble, I said:

'Princess, I've heard that, though we're not acquainted, I've had the misfortune to earn your displeasure, and that you've found me impertinent. Can this be true?'

'And now you want to confirm me in my opinion?' she replied with an ironic look that actually goes very well with her mobile features.

'If I've had the effrontery to offend you in any way, then please permit me to have the even greater effrontery to ask your pardon. Really, I should very much like to prove that you were wrong about me.'

'You'd find that rather difficult,' she said.

'Why is that?'

'Because you don't call on us, and these balls are unlikely to be very frequent.'

So their doors are shut to me for ever, I thought.

'You know, Princess,' I said, with some annoyance. 'You should never reject a penitent sinner. Despair might make him twice as bad as he was before, and then . . .'

Guffaws and whispers near by made me break off and look

round. A few yards away there was a group of men, among them the dragoon captain who had declared hostile intentions against the charming princess. He was looking very pleased about something, rubbing his hands and laughing and winking at the others. Then a red-faced fellow with long whiskers wearing a tail-coat detached himself from the group and walked unsteadily towards Princess Mary. He was drunk. He stopped in front of the embarrassed princess, put his hands behind his back and fixed her with his dull grey eyes.

'*Permettez* . . .' he began in a cracked falsetto. 'Oh, hang it all – look here, I want to dance the mazurka with you . . .'

'What is it you want?' she asked, her voice trembling. She looked round beseechingly, but unfortunately her mother was nowhere near and none of the men she knew were at hand. One of her adjutant friends, I fancy, did see what was happening, but hid in the crowd to avoid being involved in a scene.

'Well, what about it?' asked the drunk, with a wink to the dragoon captain, who was making signs to egg him on. 'Do you mean you don't want to? Then again I have the honour . . . to ask you *pour mazure*. . . . Maybe you think I'm drunk? Doesn't matter! Improves my dancing, believe me . . .'

I could see she was on the point of fainting from terror and indignation. I went up to the drunk fellow, gripped him firmly by the arm and looked him hard in the face. I then asked him to leave, since, I said, the princess had long promised to dance the mazurka with me.

'Too bad. . . . Some other time,' he said, laughing, and went off to his abashed companions, who at once led him away into the next room.

I was rewarded with a marvellous, heart-felt look of gratitude.

The princess went up to her mother and told her all about it, and the old princess sought me out in the crowd to thank me.

She told me she knew my mother and was on friendly terms with half a dozen of my aunts.

'I can't think how it is we've not met before,' she added. 'But you must admit that it's all your fault. You're so aloof, I've never known anything like it. I hope your spleen will be dispelled by the atmosphere of my drawing-room. Do you think it might?'

I replied with one of those stock phrases which everyone must have ready for such occasions.

The quadrilles went on for hours, but at last the orchestra struck up the mazurka, and Princess Mary and I sat down.

I made no allusion to the drunk, or to my previous behaviour or Grushnitsky. She gradually got over the effects of the unpleasant scene, and her face brightened up. She bantered charmingly and talked in a lively, natural, unpretentiously witty way. Some of her remarks were quite profound. In a muddled sentence I let her know that I had long been attracted to her. She inclined her head and blushed slightly. Then she looked up at me with her velvet eyes and said, with a forced laugh:

'You're a strange man.'

'I didn't want to be introduced to you,' I went on, 'because you have so many admirers I was afraid of being lost in the crowd.'

'You needn't have feared that. They're all exceedingly dull.'

'What, all of them? Do you really mean that?'

She looked at me closely, as though trying to recall something, then again blushed slightly and said emphatically:

'Yes, every one.'

'Even my friend Grushnitsky?' I asked.

'Oh, is he a friend of yours?' she said, with some uncertainty.

'Yes, he is.'

'Well, naturally, I wouldn't class him as dull . . .'

'But you would class him as unlucky!' I laughed.

'Certainly. Do you find that amusing? I wish you were in his place.'

'What's wrong with it? I was a cadet myself once, and I think it was the best time of my life.'

'Is he a cadet then?' she asked hastily. 'I always thought . . .'

'What?'

'Oh, nothing. Who is that lady?'

The conversation took another direction and the subject was dropped.

The mazurka ended and we parted – until our next meeting. The ladies went home. As I went in to supper, I bumped into Werner.

'Aha!' he said. 'So much for you! The man who wasn't going to meet the princess except by saving her from certain death!'

'I did better,' I said. 'I saved her from fainting at a ball.'

'What happened? Tell me about it.'

'No. You're such a master of guesswork, fathom it out for yourself.'

23 May

I was walking on the boulevard at about seven o'clock, when Grushnitsky spotted me in the distance and came over. His eyes were shining with an absurd look of rapture. He shook me warmly by the hand and said in a tragic voice:

'Pechorin, my thanks! You know what I mean?'

'No, I don't. But whatever it is, don't bother to thank me,' I said, not having any good deed on my conscience.

'What? But what about yesterday? You can't have forgotten. Mary has told me everything.'

'Do you share everything with her now, then? Even gratitude?'

'Look,' he said, very dignified. 'If you wish to remain my friend, kindly refrain from making fun of my love. Do you understand, I love her madly . . . and I think, I hope, she loves me too. I want to ask you a favour. You'll be visiting them this evening – will you promise to take note of all she does? I know you're more experienced in these matters and know more about women than I do. Women! Who can understand them? Their smile says one thing, their eyes another, their words lead you on with promises, but their tone of voice repulses you. One moment they guess your innermost thoughts, and the next they can't understand the most obvious hints. Take the princess, for example. Her eyes were full of feeling when she looked at me yesterday, but today they're dull and cold.'

I suggested that it might be the effect of the waters.

'You always see the worst side of things,' he said scornfully. 'Materialist! Still, let's talk of something more material.'

Pleased with this feeble pun, he quite cheered up.

Between eight and nine o'clock we went together to Princess Ligovskoy's. I saw Vera sitting at her window as we passed her house, and we exchanged a fleeting glance. Soon after we arrived she came into the drawing-room and the princess introduced me to her, saying she was a relative.

We had tea. There were a lot of guests, and the conversation was general. I tried to make myself agreeable to the old princess with my banter and several times had her laughing heartily. Once or twice Princess Mary was inclined to laugh as well, but controlled herself in order to keep up the pose she has adopted. She thinks that languor suits her, and she may well be right. Grushnitsky seems very pleased that she is immune to my gaiety.

After tea we all went into the drawing-room. As I passed Vera I asked her if she was satisfied with my obedience, and she gave me a loving look of gratitude. I'm used to these looks now, though once they were the light of my life.

Princess Ligovskoy made Mary sit at the piano, and everyone asked her to sing, though I kept quiet and took advantage of the commotion to move to a window with Vera. She wanted to tell me something very important for both of us – pure nonsense, as it turned out.

Princess Mary was annoyed by my indifference. I could tell by the flashing look of anger she gave me. How well I understand the expressive silence, the emphatic terseness of this language of looks.

She began singing. Her voice isn't bad, but she doesn't sing well – not that I listened. Grushnitsky, though, stood facing her, with his elbows on the piano, feasting his eyes on her and muttering all the time *'Charmant! Délicieux!'*

'Listen,' said Vera. 'I don't want you to meet my husband, but you simply must make the princess like you. You'll find it easy enough, you can do anything you want to. This is the only place where we'll see each other.'

'The only place?'

She blushed.

'You know I'm your slave,' she said. 'I never could resist you, though I shall suffer for it and you'll stop loving me. I want at least to keep my good name . . . not for my sake, you know that. . . . Oh, please, please don't torment me the way you used to, making me doubt you and pretending not to care. I may die soon. Every day I feel myself getting weaker, but I still don't think of the life to come, I think only of you. You men don't know the joy that a look or a touch of the hand can give. . . . Believe me, it's true. When I hear your voice I have a feeling of utter bliss that no kisses, however passionate, could ever give.'

By this time Princess Mary had stopped singing, and there

was a murmur of praise. I went up to her after everyone else and complimented her rather casually on her voice. She pulled a face, pouting her lower lip.

'Since you weren't even listening, I'm all the more flattered,' she said, with a mock curtsy. 'Perhaps you don't like music?'

'On the contrary, I do. Especially after dinner.'

'Mr Grushnitsky is right when he says your tastes are very prosaic – I see that music only appeals to you gastronomically.'

'You're wrong again. I'm no gourmet, in fact I've got a terrible digestion, but music after dinner sends me to sleep, and it's healthy to sleep – so music appeals to me medically. But in the evening it upsets me and makes me too sad or too jolly, and that's rather a bore when there's no special reason for it. Anyway, it's absurd to be sad in company, and it isn't proper to be too high-spirited . . .'

She walked away before I'd finished, and sat down by Grushnitsky. They embarked on a sentimental conversation, but though she tried to look as though she was listening, her answers to his sage remarks seemed rather vague and inappropriate, for now and then he looked at her in surprise, trying to work out the reason for her agitated, restless look.

But I see what your game is, Princess, so beware! You want to pay me back, to wound my pride, but you won't succeed. Declare war on me, and I'll show you no mercy.

I tried to break into their conversation several times during the evening, but she greeted my remarks with reserve, and in the end I withdrew, pretending to be annoyed. She was triumphant, Grushnitsky too. Enjoy your triumph while you can, my friends – it'll be short-lived.

What will the outcome be? I've a good idea. With all the women I've ever met I've known for sure if they would love me or not.

I spent the rest of the evening with Vera and had my fill of talking over old times. I really can't think why she is so fond of me, especially since she's the only woman who's ever properly understood me and all my petty weaknesses and unhealthy passions. Can evil be so attractive?

I left at the same time as Grushnitsky. He took my arm when we were outside, then, after a long pause, said:

'Well, what do you think?'

I felt like telling him he was an idiot, but restrained myself and merely shrugged my shoulders.

29 May

The last few days I've stuck firmly to my plan. Princess Mary is beginning to enjoy talking to me. I've told her some of the strange adventures I've had and she's coming to regard me as someone out of the ordinary. I make fun of everything, feelings especially, and this is beginning to alarm her. When I'm there, she doesn't venture into any sentimental discussions with Grushnitsky, and several times she's smiled ironically at things he's said. However, when Grushnitsky comes up to her, I always look resigned and leave them to themselves. The first time I did so she was pleased, or tried to pretend she was. The second time she was annoyed with me. The third time with Grushnitsky.

'You think very little of yourself,' she told me yesterday. 'Why do you think I prefer Grushnitsky's company to yours?'

I said I was sacrificing my own pleasure for the happiness of a friend.

'You're sacrificing mine as well,' she retorted.

I gazed at her with a serious look on my face – and then went the whole day without speaking to her. Last night she looked pensive, this morning at the well even more so. When I came along she was vaguely listening to Grushnitsky rhapsodizing about nature, but as soon as she saw me she started laughing, quite inappropriately, and pretended not to notice me. I walked on and watched her surreptitiously. Twice she turned away from Grushnitsky and yawned. No doubt about it, she's fed up with him. I'll go two more days without speaking to her.

3 June

I often wonder why I'm trying so hard to win the love of a girl I have no desire to seduce and whom I'd never marry. Why this womanish coquetry? Vera loves me more than Princess Mary will ever love anybody. If she were some unattainable beauty I might have been attracted by the difficulty of the undertaking. But that isn't the case, so it can't be that restless urge for love we suffer from in youth, that drives us from one woman to the next till we meet one who can't abide us. That's when our constancy begins, our true never-ending love that might be described mathematically by a line stretching from a point into space. The reason for this endlessness is simple: we can never attain our goal – our end, that is.

Why do I bother? Is it envy of Grushnitsky? Poor fellow, he's got nothing to envy. Or am I possessed by that sordid, irresistible urge which makes us destroy another's fond illusions for the petty satisfaction of saying to him, when he asks in desperation what he *can* believe in: 'My dear fellow, the same thing happened to me, but, as you see, I dine well, sup well, enjoy a good night's sleep and hope to die peacefully and without complaint.'

And yet there's boundless pleasure to be had in taking possession of a young, fresh-blossomed heart. It's like a flower that breathes its sweetest scent to the first rays of the sun. You must pluck it at once, breathe in its scent and cast it on the roadway to be picked up, perchance, by another. I've an insatiable craving inside me that consumes everything and makes me regard the sufferings and joys of others only in their relationship to me, as food to sustain my spiritual powers.

I'm no longer capable of losing my head in love. Ambition has been crushed in me by circumstances, but it comes out in another way, for ambition is nothing more than a lust for power and my chief delight is to dominate those around me. To inspire in others love, devotion, fear – isn't that the first symptom and the supreme triumph of power? To cause another person suffering or joy, having no right to do so – isn't that the sweetest food of pride? What is happiness but gratified pride? If I thought myself better and more powerful than everyone else in the world, I should be happy. If everyone loved me I should find inexhaustible founts of love within myself. Evil begets evil. The first time we suffer, we see the pleasure to be had from torturing others. The idea of evil cannot enter a man's mind without his wanting to fulfil it in practice. Someone has said that ideas are organic creations, that the moment they are conceived they have form, this form being action. The most active man is the one who conceives most ideas, and so a genius stuck in an office chair must either die or go mad, and, in the same way, a man of strong physique who leads a sedentary and temperate life will die of apoplexy.

Passions are merely ideas in their initial stage. They are the property of youth, and anyone who expects to feel their thrill throughout his life is a fool. Tranquil rivers often begin as roaring waterfalls, but no river leaps and foams all the way to the sea. Tranquillity, however, is often a sign of great, if hidden, power. Intensity and depth of feeling and thought preclude wild outbursts of passion; in sorrow and joy the soul takes careful stock of every situation, and sees that so it must be. It knows that without storms the constant heat of the sun would dry it up. It gets steeped in its own existence, coddles and chides itself like a loved child. Only this higher state of self-knowledge can give man a true appreciation of divine justice.

Reading over this page, I see that I've wandered a long way from the point. It doesn't matter. After all, I'm writing this journal for myself, and anything I care to put in it will one day be a precious memory for me.

*

Grushnitsky came in and threw his arms round me – he's got his commission. We had some champagne, then Werner arrived.

'I won't congratulate you,' he said to Grushnitsky.

'Why not?'

'Because you look very well in your private's greatcoat, and you've got to admit that a line officer's uniform made by the local tailor isn't going to do anything for you at all. Don't you see? Up to now you've been an exception, but now you'll be just one of the common run.'

'Say what you like, Doctor, but I'm delighted just the same,' said Grushnitsky, adding in a whisper to me: 'He doesn't know what hopes these epaulettes give me. These wonderful epaulettes, with their stars, their lode-stars! Yes, now I am utterly happy.'

I asked if he would join us on the walk to the chasm.

'No fear,' he said. 'I'm not going to let the princess see me before my uniform is ready.'

'Shall I tell her about your good fortune?'

'No, please don't. I'd like it to be a surprise.'

'Tell me, though – how do things stand between you two?' I said.

He was confused and looked thoughtful. He hadn't the face to brag and lie, as he'd have liked to, but at the same time it was humiliating to admit the truth.

'What do you think?' I asked. 'Is she in love with you?'

'In love with me? Really, Pechorin, what ideas you have! How could it happen so quickly? Anyway, even if she is in love, no respectable woman would ever say so.'

'Oh, fine. And I suppose you think a respectable man must keep quiet about his love too?'

'Come now, my dear fellow. There's a way for everything. There's a lot you can guess without being told.'

'True. But the love we see in a woman's eyes commits her to nothing, while words . . . . But have a care, Grushnitsky. She's making a fool of you.'

'What, she?' he exclaimed, looking heavenwards and smiling complacently. 'I pity you, Pechorin.'

With that he left.

In the evening a large party set off on a walk to the chasm. Many local scholars consider this chasm to be, in fact, the crater of an extinct volcano. It is situated on the slopes of Mashuk, three-quarters of a mile from the town. A narrow track leads up to it through scrub and rocks.

Going up the hill, I gave my arm to Princess Mary, and she held on to it for the rest of the walk. First, we talked scandal. I went through all our acquaintances, present and absent, pointing out their comic features, then their bad ones. I was in a jaundiced mood, and though I began in jest, I was being really spiteful at the end. She was amused to begin with, but then frightened.

'You're a dangerous man,' she said. 'I'd rather fall victim to a cut-throat's knife in the forest than to your tongue. Seriously, though, if you ever decide to speak ill of me, I'd rather you took a knife and killed me. I fancy you'd not find it all that hard.'

'Do you think I'm like a murderer, then?'

'No, you're worse.'

I thought for a moment, then said with a show of deep emotion:

'Yes, that's been my lot ever since I was a boy. Everyone saw in my face evil traits that I didn't possess. But they assumed I did, and so they developed. I was modest, and was accused of being deceitful, so I kept to myself. I had a strong sense of good and evil; instead of kindness I received nothing but insults, so I grew resentful. I was sullen, while other children were gay and talkative. I felt superior to them, and was set beneath them, so I became jealous. I was ready to love the whole world, but no one understood me, so I learned to hate. I spent my blighted youth in conflict with myself and the world. Fearing ridicule, I hid my best feelings deep within me, and there they died. I spoke the truth, but no one believed me, so I took to deceit. Knowing the world and the mainsprings of society, I became adept at the art of living. Yet I saw that others were happy without that art, enjoying for nothing the advantages I'd worked so hard to gain. That led me to despair, not the despair you can cure with a pistol barrel, but a cold, impotent despair that hid behind an affable exterior and a kindly smile. I became a moral cripple. One half of my soul had ceased to exist. It had withered and died, so I cut it off and cast it away. But the other half was still active, living for the service of others. But no one noticed it, because no one knew of the dead half. But now you've reminded me of it – and I've pronounced its epitaph. Many people think epitaphs ridiculous, but I don't, especially when I think what lies beneath them. But I don't ask you to share my opinion. If you find what I've said absurd, by all means laugh. I shan't be in the least offended, I assure you.'

Our eyes met at this moment. Hers were welling with tears, her hand trembled on my arm, her cheeks were flushed. She pitied me. Sympathy, that feeling which preys so easily on women, had sunk its claws into her innocent heart. The whole walk she was preoccupied and didn't even flirt with anyone, and that's a great sign.

When we reached the chasm, the ladies separated from their escorts, but she didn't leave my arm. She was unamused by the quips of the local dandies and unalarmed by the steepness of the drop beneath us, though the other girls squealed and shut their eyes.

On the way back I didn't renew our sad conversation. To my idle questions and jokes she replied tersely, inattentively. In the end I asked if she had ever been in love.

She looked hard at me, then shook her head and again was lost in thought. She obviously wanted to say something but didn't know how to begin. Her bosom heaved – small wonder, for a muslin sleeve is poor protection against the electric impulse that was passing from my arm to hers. Most love-affairs begin this way. We often fool ourselves by thinking that a woman loves us for our physical or moral qualities. They pave the way, of course, they dispose her heart to receive the sacred fire, but it's the first physical touch that really counts.

When we got back, she forced a smile and said:

'I've been very amiable today, don't you think?'

We parted.

She's dissatisfied with herself, reproaches herself for being cold. This is the first triumph, the one that counts. Tomorrow she'll want to make it up to me. But I know it all by heart – that's the bore of it.

4 June

I saw Vera today. She's jealous, and gave me hell. Apparently, Princess Mary has taken it into her head to confide in her. An excellent choice, I must say.

'I can tell the way things are going,' Vera said. 'Why don't you tell me now that you love her?'

'And what if I don't love her?' I said.

'Then why do you pursue her? Why arouse her imagination? Oh, I know you too well. Listen, if you want me to believe you, come to Kislovodsk next week. We're going there the day after tomorrow. The princess is staying on here for a while. Take the house next to ours. We'll be staying in the big house by the spring, in the mezzanine. Princess Ligovskoy will be on the floor below us. There's a house next door owned by the same man that's not been taken. Will you come?'

I promised, and the same day sent word that I wished to rent this house.

At six Grushnitsky came round with the news that his uniform would be ready tomorrow, just in time for the ball.

'At last I'm going to have a whole evening dancing with her. There are so many things I want to tell her, and now's my chance.'

'When is the ball?'

'Why, tomorrow. Surely you know that? It's a great event, being put on by the local authorities.'

'Coming for a stroll on the boulevard?' I asked.

'No fear, not in this beastly greatcoat.'

'Not so fond of it now, eh?'

I went out alone. I met Princess Mary and engaged her for the mazurka at the ball. She seemed surprised and pleased.

'I thought you only danced from necessity, like the last time,' she said, smiling very prettily.

She doesn't seem to have noticed Grushnitsky's absence.

'You'll have a pleasant surprise tomorrow,' I said.

'What's that?'

'It's a secret. You'll see for yourself at the ball.'

That evening I finished up at the Ligovskoys. The only other guests were Vera and an old man who was very entertaining. I was in a good mood and told them a number of improbable stories made up on the spur of the moment.

Princess Mary sat facing me, listening to this rubbish with such a rapt and tender expression that my conscience troubled me. What's become of her vivacity, her coquetry and capricious ways? Where are the haughty look, the disdainful smile, the detached expression?

Vera saw all this. She sat in the shadow by the window, sunk in a large armchair, looking ill and utterly miserable. I felt sorry for her.

Then I told the whole dramatic story of our relationship, of our love, naturally using fictitious names. I gave such a vivid description of my love and all its cares and raptures, and presented her character and actions in such a favourable light that she couldn't but forgive my flirting with Princess Mary.

She got up and came to sit with us and her spirits improved. It wasn't until two in the morning that we remembered the doctor's orders to go to bed at eleven.

5 June

Half an hour before the ball Grushnitsky came round, resplendent in his infantry officer's uniform. He had a *lorgnette* dangling from a bronze chain on the third button of his tunic, and wore enormous epaulettes that turned upwards like Cupid's wings, and boots that squeaked. He had his cap and brown kid gloves in his left hand and with his right kept arranging the ringlets of his carefully curled forelock. He looked pleased with himself, but somewhat diffident too. His festive appearance and grand bearing would have been enough to make me laugh outright, if that had suited my intentions.

He tossed his cap and gloves on the table and stood in front of the mirror, pulling down the tails of his tunic and straightening his dress. He wore an enormous black neckcloth on a high stiffener, the padding of which propped up his chin. He thought the inch or so of neckcloth showing above his collar wasn't enough, so tugged it up till it reached his ears. These exertions left him purple in the face, for his tunic collar was extremely tight and uncomfortable.

'I hear you've been busy making eyes at my princess lately,' he said casually, without looking at me.

'Never a dog's chance for the likes of me,' I answered, repeating the favourite saying of one of the artfullest rogues of former times, whose praises Pushkin once sang.

'Well, how do you think my uniform fits?' he asked. 'Ah, that damned Jew has made it too tight under the arms. By the way, do you have any scent?'

'Come off it,' I said. 'What do you want more scent for? You reek of rose-water as it is.'

'I don't care. Let's have some.'

He poured half a bottle down his cravat and on his handkerchief and sleeves.

'Are you going to dance?' he asked.

'I don't expect so.'

'I'm afraid I might have to lead with Mary in the mazurka, and I hardly know a single figure,' he said.

'Have you asked her for the mazurka?'

'No, I haven't yet.'

'Mind someone doesn't get in first.'

'Lord, you're right!' he said, slapping his forehead. 'Goodbye – I'll go and wait for her at the entrance.'

He snatched up his cap and hurried off.

I left half an hour later. The streets were dark and empty, but there was a crowd outside the Assembly Rooms (or tavern, if you prefer it). The windows were a blaze of lights, and strains of the regimental band came to me on the evening breeze. I walked slowly, feeling depressed.

Is it my sole function in life, I thought, to be the ruin of other people's hopes? Through all my active life fate always seems to have brought me in for the *dénouement* of other people's dramas. As if nobody could die or despair without my help. I've been the indispensable figure of the fifth act, thrust into the pitiful role of executioner or betrayer. What was fate's purpose? Perhaps I was meant to be a writer of domestic tragedies or novels of family life, or a purveyor of stories, perhaps, for the Reader's Library? How can one tell? Many people start life expecting to end up as Alexander the Great or Lord Byron, then spend their whole lives as minor civil servants.

Entering the ballroom, I took refuge among a cluster of men and sized up the situation. Grushnitsky stood by Princess Mary, talking with great fervour. She listened inattentively, looking this way and that, her fan against her lips. She looked impatient, her eyes were seeking someone. I quietly went up behind them to hear what they were saying.

'Princess, you're tormenting me,' said Grushnitsky. 'You've changed a lot since I last saw you.'

'You've changed as well,' she said, darting him a glance whose hidden mockery was lost on him.

'I change? Never! You know that's impossible. Anyone who sees you once must carry your divine image with him to the grave.'

'Oh, do stop it!'

'A short while ago you listened kindly when I said these things to you, and often too. Why won't you listen now?'

'Because I dislike repetition,' she laughed.

'Oh, I've been sadly mistaken. Fool that I was, I thought at least that with these epaulettes I'd have the right to hope. But no, I'd be better off in my contemptible greatcoat. Perhaps that was why you noticed me.'

'Indeed, I really do think your greatcoat suited you much better.'

At this point I went up and bowed to the princess. She blushed slightly, then said quickly:

'Monsieur Pechorin, don't you think Monsieur Grushnitsky looked much nicer in his grey greatcoat?'

'No, I don't agree,' I replied. 'His uniform makes him look more boyish than ever.'

This shot was too much for Grushnitsky. Like all boys, he fancies himself an old man. He thinks the deep lines of passion on his face pass muster for the stamp of age. With a furious look at me, he stamped and walked away.

'Confess, though,' I said to the princess. 'He's always been ridiculous, but it's not so long since you found him – and his greatcoat – interesting, is it?'

She looked down and made no reply.

The whole evening Grushnitsky pursued her, dancing either with her or *vis-à-vis*, devouring her with his eyes, sighing, and pestering her with pleas and reproaches. By the end of the third quadrille she hated him.

'I never expected this from you,' he said, coming up and taking me by the arm.

'Never expected what?'

'You're dancing the mazurka with her, aren't you?' he asked in a solemn voice. 'She's admitted it to me.'

'Well, what of it? It's not a secret, is it?'

'Of course not. I should have expected as much from a flirt, a minx like her. But I'll get even.'

'Why blame her? Blame it on your greatcoat or your epaulettes. She can't help it if she doesn't like you any more.'

'Then why did she raise my hopes?'

'Why did you hope? I can understand someone wanting a thing and trying to get it, but who ever hopes?'

'You've won your bet,' he said, with a vicious smile. 'Only not quite.'

The mazurka began. Grushnitsky picked Princess Mary every time, and she was constantly chosen by others too, so there was obviously a plot against me. So much the better – she wants to talk to me and they won't let her, so she'll want to twice as badly.

I squeezed her hand a couple of times. The second occasion she drew it away without saying anything.

'I shall sleep badly tonight,' she told me at the end of the mazurka.

'That's Grushnitsky's fault.'

'Oh no, it's not,' she said.

She looked so sad and thoughtful that I promised myself I'd kiss her hand before the evening was out.

People began to leave. As I handed the princess into her carriage, I quickly pressed her tiny hand to my lips. It was dark, so no one could see.

I went back to the ballroom, well pleased with myself.

The young bloods were having supper at the big table. Grushnitsky was there. Evidently they were talking about me, for when I went in they all stopped. A lot of them have it in for me since the last ball, especially the dragoon captain, and now they seem to be ganging up against me in earnest, with Grushnitsky as ringleader. He's looking very proud and courageous.

I'm delighted. I love enemies, though not in the Christian way. Being always on the alert, catching their every glance, the hidden meaning of every word, guessing their next step, confounding their plans, pretending to be taken in and then with one fell blow wrecking the whole elaborate fabric of their cunning schemes – that's what I call living!

All through supper Grushnitsky was whispering and exchanging winks with the dragoon captain.

6 June

This morning Vera left for Kislovodsk with her husband. I met their carriage on my way to the Ligovskoys. She nodded to me. She looked reproachful.

Whose fault is it? Why won't she give me an opportunity of seeing her alone? Love is like fire – without fuel it dies. Perhaps jealousy will succeed where pleas have failed.

I spent a whole hour at the Ligovskoys, but Mary didn't appear because she is unwell. She wasn't out on the boulevard this evening either. The gang were all there, armed with *lorgnettes*. They look menacing. I'm glad Princess Mary is ill, or else they might have insulted her in some way. Grushnitsky is looking dishevelled and has a desperate air. He seems genuinely put out, especially on account of his wounded vanity. But then, in some people even despair is amusing.

I reached home with the feeling that something was missing. *I hadn't seen her. She's ill.* Perhaps I've fallen in love myself? No, that's nonsense.

7 June

At eleven this morning (the hour when Princess Ligovskoy is usually sweating it out in the Yermolov baths) I passed their house. Princess Mary was sitting at the window, lost in thought. On seeing me, she jumped up.

I went into the hall. There were no servants about, so I took advantage of the easy-going customs of these parts and made my way to the drawing-room unannounced.

Princess Mary stood by the piano. One hand, trembling slightly, rested on the back of an armchair. Her charming face looked mat and pale. I went slowly up to her.

'Are you angry with me?' I asked.

She looked up and gave me a long, languid gaze, then shook her head. She wanted to speak, but couldn't. Tears filled her eyes, and, covering her face, she sank into the chair.

'What's wrong?' I asked, taking her hand.

'You don't respect me. . . . Oh, leave me alone!'

I took a few paces. She sat up straight in her chair, her eyes shining. I stopped, with my hand on the door-handle.

'Forgive me, Princess,' I said. 'I behaved like a madman. It won't happen again. There's no reason for you to know what's been going on in my heart. You'll never know, and so much the better for you. Good-bye.'

As I left I thought I heard her crying.

I wandered about in the neighbourhood of Mashuk till evening. I was extremely tired, and when I got home I fell on my bed in a state of utter exhaustion.

Werner dropped in to see me.

'Is it true you're going to marry Princess Mary?' he asked.

'Why do you ask?'

'It's all over the town. All my patients are full of this important news. And there's no one like my patients for knowing everything.'

Grushnitsky is up to his tricks, I thought.

'To prove how untrue these rumours are, Doctor, I'll let you into a secret. I'm leaving for Kislovodsk tomorrow.'

'Princess Ligovskoy as well?'

'No. She's here for another week.'

'You can't be getting married then!'

'Come now, Doctor. Look at me. Do I look like a man who's going to get married?'

'I'm not saying you do. But,' he added, with a sly smile, 'there are cases . . . when an honourable man is obliged to marry, and some fond mothers don't prevent this happening, to say the least. So I advise you as a friend to watch your step. The air in these spas is extremely dangerous. I've seen a lot of young men who deserved a better fate going straight from here to the altar. Would you believe it – they even tried to marry me off once! It was one of those provincial mothers. Her daughter was a pale creature, and I had the misfortune to say that marriage would soon bring the colour back to her cheeks, whereupon the mother wept with gratitude and offered me the girl's hand and her entire fortune – fifty serfs, I think it was. But I said I wasn't cut out for it.'

Werner left, fully convinced that he had saved me by his warning.

From what he had said I saw that ugly rumours were being put about the town concerning Princess Mary and myself. Grushnitsky won't get away with that!

10 June

I've been in Kislovodsk three days now. Each day I see Vera at the well and out walking. When I wake up in the morning, I sit by the window and look at her balcony through my glass. She is already dressed, waiting for the prearranged signal. We meet as though by chance in the garden that goes down from our houses to the well. She has got back her colour and strength in this invigorating mountain air. It's not for nothing that they call Narzan 'the champions' spring'. The local people claim that the air in Kislovodsk puts one in the mood for love, and that love affairs that begin at the foot of Mashuk reach happy endings here. There is certainly an all-pervading air of solitude about the place. Everything is mysterious: the murky shade of the lime walks above the foaming torrent that roars down from ledge to ledge, cutting its way through the green-clad hills, the ravines, full of mist and silence, that branch off here in all directions, the freshness of the scented air, laden with the perfume of tall southern grasses and white acacia, and the ceaseless, lusciously soporific sound of icy streams that meet at the foot of the valley and merrily race one another till at last they rush into the Podkumok. On this side the gorge is broader, opening out into a green valley, with a dusty road winding along it. Every time I look at this road I fancy I see a carriage with a rosy face looking through the window. Many carriages have passed along the road, but not yet this one.

The suburb beyond the fort is now a populous district. There's a restaurant on the hill a few yards from my lodging, and in the evenings its lights glitter through the double row of poplars. The shouting and clinking of glasses goes on till all hours of the night.

More Kakhetian wine and mineral water are drunk here than anywhere else in the world.

> Many are fond of combining these two,
> But it's something that I prefer never to do.

Grushnitsky and his gang have rowdy parties in the tavern each day. He scarcely bows to me now.

He only arrived yesterday and has already quarrelled with three old fellows who wanted to go before him at the baths. No doubt about it – misfortune is making him aggressive!

11 June

They've arrived at last. I heard their carriage as I sat at my window, and my heart missed a beat. What does it mean? Can I be in love? The stupid way I'm made, it's the sort of thing you might expect.

I dined with them. The princess looks very tenderly at me and keeps close to her daughter – a bad sign. As for Vera, I'm in the happy state of having made her jealous of Princess Mary.

What won't a woman do to hurt a rival! I remember one woman who loved me simply because I was in love with someone else. There's nothing more paradoxical than the female mind, and you can never convince a woman of anything – you have to arrange matters so that they convince themselves. The chain of reasoning they employ to overcome their own prejudices is extremely original, and if you want to master their dialectic you have to turn all the textbook rules of logic upside-down. For example, a normal approach would be: 'This man loves me, but I'm married, so I mustn't love him'. But a woman's approach would be: 'I mustn't love him, because I'm married, but he loves me, so . . .' I have to use dots here, for now the voice of reason is silent, and it's mainly the tongue, eyes and heart (if there is one) which do all the talking.

If a woman ever chances to read these notes there'll be outraged cries of 'Slander!'

Since poets began writing and women began reading them (for which our heartfelt thanks), they have been called angels so often that, in their simplicity, they've come to accept this compliment as the truth. They forget that the same poets – in return for money – acclaimed Nero as a demigod.

I really oughtn't to be so biting about them, I who have loved nothing in the world but them and have always been ready to sacrifice for them peace of mind, ambition, even life itself. But it's not from pique or injured vanity that I attempt to pluck from them the magic veil that needs a practised eye to see through. No, all I say is just the result of

> The intellect's cold observations,
> The bitter record of the heart.

Women should wish all men to know them as well as I do, for since I stopped fearing them and understood their petty weaknesses, I've loved them a hundred times more dearly.

Incidentally, the other day Werner compared women to the enchanted forest in Tasso's *Jerusalem Delivered*.

'No sooner do you approach,' said he, 'than untold horrors swarm on you from every side – duty, pride, respectability, public opinion, ridicule, disdain. You mustn't take any notice of them, but just walk straight ahead. The monsters gradually vanish, and before you opens a peaceful, sunny glade, with the green myrtle blossoming in its midst. But all is lost, if your heart quakes and you turn back at the beginning.'

12 June

This evening was rich in events.

Two or three miles from Kislovodsk, in the gorge of the Podkumok, there's a rock called The Ring. It stands high on a hill and forms a natural gateway, through which the setting sun casts a last fiery glance at the world. A large party of us rode out to watch the sunset through this stone window, though, in fact, nobody gave much thought to the sun.

I rode by Princess Mary, and on the way home we had to ford the Podkumok. Any mountain stream is dangerous to ford, even the shallowest of them, chiefly because of the way the bed shifts. It's like a kaleidoscope, changing every day with the force of the current, and where there is a rock one day, there will be a hole the next. I took the princess's horse by the bridle and led it into the water. It was only knee-deep, and we started slowly across, moving diagonally upstream. It's a well-known fact that you should never look down at the water when crossing a swift-flowing stream, or you'll feel giddy. I forgot to warn her about this.

When we were in mid-stream, where the current was fastest, she suddenly swayed in the saddle.

'I don't feel well,' she muttered feebly.

I quickly leaned across and put my arm round her supple waist.

'Look up,' I whispered. 'It's all right. Just don't be afraid. I'm here.'

She felt better and tried to free herself from my arm, but I tightened my grip on her soft, tender waist. My face was almost touching hers, and I could feel the warmth of her burning cheek.

'What are you doing to me?' she cried. 'Oh, God!'

Disregarding her trembling and confusion, I touched my lips on her tender cheek. She quivered, but said nothing. We were riding behind the others, so no one saw us. When we came out on the far bank, the whole party set off at a trot. The princess held her horse back, and I stayed by her. She was obviously disturbed by my silence, but I vowed that, out of curiosity, I would say nothing. I wanted to see how she would extricate herself from this awkward situation.

'Either you despise me or else you love me very much,' she said.

There were tears in her voice.

'Perhaps you wish to make fun of me, to rouse my feelings and then desert me, but that would be so base and vile, the very idea. . . . No,' she added, her voice tender and trusting, 'there's really no reason why you shouldn't respect me, is there? I must forgive your boldness, for I allowed it to happen. Won't you say something? Won't you answer me? I want to hear your voice.'

There was so much feminine impatience in these last words that I couldn't help smiling. Luckily it was getting dark.

I made no reply.

'You are silent?' she said. 'Perhaps you want me to say first that I love you?'

I said nothing.

'Is that what you want?' she asked, turning sharply towards me. There was something terrifying in the resolute expression of her face and voice.

I shrugged my shoulders.

'Why should I?' I answered.

She lashed her horse and galloped full tilt along the narrow, perilous track. It happened so quickly that I barely managed to catch up with her, and by then she had rejoined the main party.

All the way home she talked and laughed. There was a feverish quality in her movements. She ignored me completely. Everyone noticed her unusually high spirits, and her mother was inwardly delighted to see her daughter like this, though in fact it was just a state of nerves. She'll be awake all night crying. The thought gives me enormous satisfaction. There are times when I can understand the Vampire, and yet I still pass for a decent fellow and try my best to be thought so.

The ladies dismounted and went into the Ligovskoys. I was feeling on edge, so galloped into the hills to clear my head of the thoughts that crowded in on me. There was a heady coolness in the dewy evening air. The moon was rising over the dark peaks, and my unshod horse's every step echoed dully through the silence of the valleys. I gave my horse a drink by a waterfall, took a couple of deep breaths of the cool southern night air and set off home.

I went by way of the suburb. The lights were going out in the windows, and the sentries on the wall of the fort exchanged long drawn out shouts with Cossacks in the neighbouring pickets.

I noticed one house built on the edge of a ravine which was particularly brilliantly lit. Occasional shouts and a babble of voices told me it was an officers' drinking party.

I dismounted and crept up to a window. One shutter was not properly closed and I could see the people inside and hear what they said. They were talking about me. The dragoon captain, flushed with wine, banged his fist on the table for order.

'Gentlemen!' he said. 'It's just not good enough. We've got to teach Pechorin a lesson. These Petersburg puppies get above themselves unless you slap them down. Just because he's got clean gloves and polished boots he fancies he's the only society man among us.'

'Yes, with that superior smile of his!' said another. 'Actually, I think he's a coward, nothing more than a coward.'

'I think so too,' said Grushnitsky. 'He likes passing everything off as a joke. I once said things to him anyone else would have killed me for on the spot, but he just made a joke of it. Naturally I didn't challenge him – that was up to him to do, and anyway I didn't want to get involved.'

'Grushnitsky's got it in for him because he cut him out with the princess,' remarked someone.

'That's rich!' said Grushnitsky. 'It's true, I did show some interest in her, but I soon gave up. I'm not keen to get married, and I don't believe in compromising a girl.'

'You take my word,' said the dragoon captain. 'He's a prize coward – Pechorin, I mean, not Grushnitsky. Grushnitsky's a fine fellow and my very good friend. So, gentlemen, there's nobody here who stands up for him? Nobody? So much the better. Would you like to see how brave he is? It'd be a bit of sport for us.'

'By all means. How?'

'Now, listen. Grushnitsky's got a special grievance against him, so he takes the lead. He'll take him up on some trifle and challenge him to a duel. Just a minute – this is the whole point. . . . He'll challenge him, fine. Challenge, preparations, conditions – all very solemn and awesome, I'll see to that. I'll be your second, my poor friend. All right. Only here's the catch – we won't put bullets in the pistols. I guarantee Pechorin will funk it. Damn it, I'll fix the duel at six paces. Are you with me?'

There was general agreement.

'Splendid scheme! We're game! Why not?'

'What about you, Grushnitsky?'

I waited tremulously for his reply. The thought that but for chance I might have become the laughing-stock of these fools filled me with cold malice. If Grushnitsky had refused to agree I would have embraced him, but after a short silence he rose, stretched out his hand to the captain and replied pompously:

'Very well, I agree.'

It would be hard to describe the delight of the worthy company.

I went home, stirred by two quite different emotions. The first was sorrow. Why do they hate me? I thought. What cause have they? I haven't offended anyone, have I? Or am I one of those people the very sight of whom rouses hostility? And I felt my heart slowly filling with venomous spite.

'Take care, Grushnitsky,' I said, pacing my room. 'You don't play that kind of trick on me, and you may find yourself paying dearly for going along with your stupid friends. I'm not your plaything.'

I was awake all night, and by morning I was as yellow as parchment.

I met Princess Mary at the well during the morning. She studied me closely.

'Are you ill?' she asked.

'I didn't sleep last night,' I said.

'Neither did I. I was blaming you, perhaps unfairly? Please tell me. I can forgive everything.'

'Everything?'

'Yes, everything. Only tell me the truth, please. I've thought a lot about it, I've tried to explain and justify your behaviour. Are you afraid of difficulties from my family? That doesn't matter. When they know' – her voice quivered – 'I'll talk them round. Or is it your position? Please understand, I'm ready to give up everything for the man I love. Oh, please answer me, please. Have pity on me. You don't despise me, do you?'

She seized my hand.

Her mother was walking ahead of us with Vera's husband. She saw nothing, but we were in full view of the invalids out walking, and there's no one worse than invalids for prying and gossiping about other people's affairs. I quickly withdrew my hand from her passionate grip.

'I'll tell you the whole truth,' I said. 'I'll not defend myself or explain my actions. I do not love you.'

Her lips paled slightly.

'Leave me,' she said, her voice barely audible.

I shrugged my shoulders, turned and walked away.

14 June

Sometimes I despise myself – perhaps that's why I despise others? I've lost my capacity for noble impulses, for I'm afraid of making a fool of myself. Anyone else would have offered the princess *son cœur et sa fortune*, but for me the word 'marriage' has a magic power. However much I loved a woman, the first hint that she expected me to marry her would banish my love for good. My heart would turn to stone, its warmth gone for ever. I'll make any sacrifice except this one. I'll hazard my life, even my honour, twenty times, but I will not sell my freedom.

Why do I value it so much? What use is it to me? What am I preparing myself for? What do I expect from the future? Absolutely nothing.

I have this innate fear, this uncanny premonition. After all, some people are unaccountably afraid of spiders, cockroaches and mice. Perhaps I should admit it – that when I was a child an old woman told my mother my fortune and said I would die through a bad wife. I was very impressed by this at the time and acquired this unconquerable aversion to marriage. Something tells me her prophecy will come true, but at least I'll do what I can to delay it.

15 June

Apfelbaum the conjurer arrived here yesterday. A long poster appeared on the door of the restaurant informing the respected public that the above-named remarkable conjurer, acrobat, alchemist and illusionist would have the honour to present a spectacular performance this day at eight o'clock p.m. in the hall of the Assembly Rooms (alias the restaurant). Tickets 2 roubles 50 copeks.

Everyone is going to watch the remarkable conjurer, and even Princess Ligovskoy has bought a ticket, although her daughter is unwell.

I walked past Vera's windows after dinner. She was sitting alone on the balcony, and a note dropped at my feet.

Come this evening after nine. Use the main stairs. My husband has gone to Pyatigorsk and won't be back till morning. The servants and maids will all be out – I've given them tickets for the show. I've done the same for the princess's servants. I'm expecting you. You must come.

Aha! I thought, things have turned my way at last.

At eight I went to see the conjurer, but it was nearly nine by the time the audience had assembled and the show began. I spotted Vera's servants and the princess's in the back rows. They were all there. Grushnitsky was sitting in the front row with his *lorgnette* and every time the conjurer wanted a handkerchief, watch, ring, and so on, he applied to him.

Grushnitsky has been cutting me for some time, and now he gave me a couple of rather insolent looks. It will all be in the record when we come to settle our account.

A little before ten I got up and left.

It was pitch black outside. The mountains were capped by cold, heavy clouds, and a dying wind rustled occasionally in the tops of the poplars round the restaurant. People crowded at the windows.

I went down the hill and, quickening my pace, turned into the gate. I had a sudden feeling there was someone following me. I stopped and looked back, but saw nothing in the darkness. Still, to be on the safe side, I walked right round the house as though I were out for a stroll. As I passed Princess Mary's windows I again heard steps behind me and a man muffled in a greatcoat ran past me. Despite this alarm, I crept to the porch and hurried up the dark stairway. The door opened, a small hand grasped mine.

'Did anyone see you?' Vera whispered, pressing herself to me.

'No, nobody.'

'Now do you believe that I love you? I was in torment making up my mind, but you can twist me any way you want.'

Her heart was thumping, her hands were like ice. She came out with a string of jealous reproaches and complaints. She wanted me to make a clean breast of everything and said she would resign herself to my being unfaithful, since all she wanted was my happiness. I didn't altogether believe her, but comforted her with vows, promises and the rest.

'So you're not going to marry Mary?' she said. 'You don't love her? But she thinks. . . . Do you know the poor girl's madly in love with you?'

*

At about two in the morning I opened the window and with two shawls knotted together let myself down from the upper balcony to the one below, steadying myself on a pillar. There was still a light in Princess Mary's room and, on impulse, I went up to her window. The curtain wasn't quite drawn, so I could peep inside. Mary was sitting on the bed, her hands folded on her lap. Her thick hair was gathered up under a lace-trimmed night-cap. She had a large crimson shawl over her shoulders and gaily-coloured Persian slippers on her tiny feet. She sat quite still, her head sunk on her breast. A book lay open on the table before her, but her fixed, sorrowful eyes seemed to be reading the same page for the hundredth time, with her thoughts far away.

At this moment someone stirred behind a bush. I leaped from the balcony on to the grass.

'Aha, got you!' cried a rough voice. 'I'll teach you to go visiting princesses at night!'

'Hold him tight!' cried a second person, springing out from the corner.

It was Grushnitsky and the dragoon captain.

I laid out the dragoon with a punch on the head and dashed into the bushes. I knew every path of these gardens on the slope opposite our houses.

'Thieves! Help!' they cried, and there was a musket shot – the smoking wad landed almost at my feet.

A minute later I was in my room, undressed and in bed. My servant scarcely had the key turned in the lock when Grushnitsky and the captain banged on my door.

'Pechorin!' roared the captain. 'Are you asleep? Are you there?'

'I'm in bed,' I called back angrily.

'Well, get up. There are thieves about, Circassians . . .'

'I've got a bad cold,' I said. 'I don't want to catch a chill.'

They went away. I shouldn't have answered and then they could have spent another hour looking for me in the garden.

Meanwhile, there was a frightful state of alarm. A Cossack came galloping down from the fort, and there was a general bustle of activity, with people searching for Circassians behind every bush – naturally without success. Many, however, were probably quite convinced that if only the garrison had shown more pluck and dash, then a good score of the raiders would have been laid low.

16 June

At the well this morning the sole subject of conversation was the night raid of the Circassians. When I'd had my quota of Narzan and taken a dozen turns along the lime walk, I met Vera's husband, just back from Pyatigorsk. He took my arm and we went to lunch at the restaurant. He was very concerned about his wife.

'She was terrified last night,' he said. 'Of course it would happen just when I was away.'

We sat down to lunch in a corner by the door into another room where a dozen of the young set had gathered. Grushnitsky was there, and once again I was destined to overhear a conversation which was to settle his fate. He'd not seen me, so I couldn't suppose he acted by design, though this only made it worse as far as I was concerned.

'Was it really Circassians, though?' someone asked. 'Did anybody see them?'

'I'll tell you the whole thing,' said Grushnitsky. 'Only please don't say I told you. What happened was this: last night a certain person, whose name I won't mention, came and told me he'd seen someone getting into the Ligovskoys' house some time after nine. The old princess was here, you will note, but the daughter was at home. So we went and waited for this lucky fellow under her window.'

I confess I was alarmed. Though my companion was engrossed in his lunch, he might well hear some rather distasteful facts if Grushnitsky happened to have realized the truth. But Grushnitsky was blinded by jealousy and never suspected what had really happened.

'So along we went,' he continued. 'We took a gun loaded with blank, just to put the wind up him. We waited in the garden till two and then somebody came down from the balcony, I don't know where from – it wasn't through the window because it didn't open. He probably came out of the glass door behind the pillar. Anyway, down he came. What do you think of the princess now, eh? These Moscow princesses really are the limit. What can you believe after this, eh? We tried to grab him, but he got away and hared off among the bushes. That was when I fired at him.'

There were incredulous murmurs.

'So you don't believe me?' said Grushnitsky. 'Well, I give you my solemn word of honour it's the absolute truth. If you like I can prove it by telling you the man's name.'

'Come on then, tell us. Who is he?' they cried.

'Pechorin.'

At that moment he looked up and saw me facing him in the doorway. He flushed crimson. I went up to him and said slowly and clearly:

'I'm sorry I didn't come in before you staked your honour on this filthy slander. I could have stopped you behaving despicably for once in your life.'

Grushnitsky leaped up with a show of fury, and I continued in the same tone:

'I ask you to take back what you've said this instant. You know very well it's untrue, and I don't think a woman's indifference to your brilliant qualities merits this terrible revenge. Think seriously what it means. You stand by what you said, and you lose the right to be called a man of honour – and are in danger of your life.'

Grushnitsky stood in front of me, eyes downcast, in a state of violent emotion. The struggle between conscience and conceit didn't last long, however. The dragoon captain, sitting next to him, nudged him with his elbow. Grushnitsky started, and then, with his eyes still lowered, hastily replied:

'When I say a thing, sir, I mean it and am ready to repeat it. I'm not afraid of your threats and I'll go to any lengths . . .'

'That you've already demonstrated,' I retorted icily.

Then, taking the dragoon captain's arm, I left the room.

'What do you want?' asked the captain.

'You're Grushnitsky's friend,' I said. 'I presume you'll be his second?'

He made a solemn bow.

'You're quite correct,' he said. 'In fact, I'm obliged to be his second, since your insult to him is also an insult to me – I was with him last night in the garden,' he added, pulling his drooping figure erect.

'Ah, so it was you I gave that clumsy punch on the head?' I said.

His face turned yellow, then blue with stifled rage. I pretended not to notice his fury and said:

'I shall have the honour to send you my second today.'

I met Vera's husband on the restaurant steps. He seemed to be waiting for me and grasped my hand in a state of near rapture. When he spoke there were tears in his eyes.

'Noble fellow!' he said. 'I heard it all. That ungrateful scoundrel! What decent man's going to have him in his house after that? Thank heaven I have no daughters! You'll get your reward, though, from the lady you're risking your life for. In the meantime you can rely on my discretion. I was young myself once and a military man too. I know one mustn't interfere in these affairs. Good-bye.'

The poor fool. He's glad he has no daughters!

I went straight to Werner's and found him in. I told him the whole story, all about me and Vera and Princess Mary, and about hearing the conversation when they were planning to make me fight a duel with pistols loaded with blank. They wanted to make a fool of me then, but now it was past a joke. They probably never expected it to turn out like this.

The doctor agreed to be my second, and I gave him instructions about the terms of the duel. He was to insist on the utmost secrecy, for though I'm prepared to risk being killed, I'm not at all inclined to ruin my future prospects in this world.

I went home. An hour later Werner was back from his errand.

'There's a plot against you, all right,' he said. 'I found that dragoon captain at Grushnitsky's, and another fellow, I can't remember his name. I stopped a moment in the hall to take off my galoshes and heard them arguing and making a frightful row. "I absolutely refuse," Grushnitsky was saying. "He's insulted me in public. Before it was different." "You won't be concerned in it," said the captain. "I'll see to everything. I've been a second five times and know how to fix it. I've got it all worked out, so just leave it to me. There's no harm in giving him a fright, and why risk danger yourself if you don't have to?"

'I went in at this point and they all stopped talking. Our discussions took some time, but this is what we decided on in the end. There's a lonely gorge three miles or so from here. They're going there at four o'clock tomorrow morning and we'll leave half an hour after them. You'll fire at six paces – that was Grushnitsky's own idea – and if either of you is killed we put it down to the Circassians. Now, I'll tell you what I suspect. I think they – the seconds – have changed their original plan and are going to load Grushnitsky's pistol with ball, but not yours. It smacks of murder, but this is war, Asian war at that, and no holds are barred. Grushnitsky seems to have a bit more decency than his friends, though. Well, what do you think? Should we let them know we're on to it?'

'Not on your life, Doctor. Don't you worry, they won't get the better of me.'

'What are you going to do?'

'That's my secret.'

'Well, see you don't get caught. It's at six paces, you know.'

'Doctor,' I said, 'I'll expect you tomorrow at four. The horses will be ready. Good-bye.'

I stayed in till evening, locked in my room. A servant came from the Ligovskoys' asking me to call on the old princess, but I gave orders to say I was unwell.

It's two in the morning. I can't sleep, though I ought to get some sleep if I'm to have a steady hand in the morning. Though it's difficult to miss at six paces. Ah, Grushnitsky, your ruse won't work. The roles will be reversed – it'll be I who studies your pale face for the marks of hidden fear. Why did you choose these fatal six paces? Do you think I'll meekly be your target? Oh no, we'll draw lots and then ... then ... What if your luck holds out against mine? What if my star lets me down at last? It might well do, for it's pandered to my whims long enough, and there's no more constancy in heaven than on earth.

What if it does? If I die, I die. It will be small loss to the world, and I've had about enough of it myself. I'm like a man yawning at a ball who doesn't go home to bed because his carriage hasn't come. But when it arrives – farewell!

I've been going over my past, and I can't help wondering

why I've lived, for what purpose I was born. There must have been some purpose, I must have had some high object in life, for I feel unbounded strength within me. But I never discovered it and was carried away by the allurements of empty, un-rewarding passions. I was tempered in their flames and came out cold and hard as steel, but I'd lost for ever the fire of noble endeavour, that finest flower of life. How many times since then have I been the axe in the hands of fate? Like an engine of execution, I've descended on the heads of the condemned, often without malice, but always without pity. My love has brought no one happiness, for I've never sacrificed a thing for those I've loved. I've loved for myself, for my own pleasure, I've only tried to satisfy a strange inner need. I've fed on their feelings, love, joys and sufferings, and always wanted more. I'm like a starving man who falls asleep exhausted and sees rich food and sparkling wines before him. He rapturously falls on these phantom gifts of the imagination and feels better, but the moment he wakes up his dream disappears and he's left more hungry and desperate than before.

And perhaps tomorrow I'll die, and then there'll be no one who could ever really understand me. Some will think me worse, others better than in fact I am. Some will say I was a good fellow, others that I was a swine. Neither will be right. So why bother to live? One just goes on living out of curiosity, waiting for something new. It's absurd and annoying.

I've now been six weeks here in the fort at N—. Maxim Maximych has gone out hunting, and I'm alone, sitting by the window. There are grey clouds right down to the foot of the mountains and the sun is just a yellow blob shining through the mist. It's cold, and there's a whistling wind that rattles the shutters. I'm bored, so I'll go on with my journal that's been interrupted by so many strange events.

It's funny to read over the last page. I thought I might die. But that was impossible – even now I've not yet drained my cup of suffering, and feel I still have long to live.

How clearly and distinctly I remember the past. Time hasn't erased a single line or tint from my memories. I remember not sleeping a wink the night before the duel. I couldn't write for long, for I had a strange feeling of disquiet. I spent an hour pacing the room, then sat down and opened a novel that lay on the table. It was Walter Scott's *Old Mortality*. At first it was an effort to read, but I was soon carried away by the magic of the tale. The Scottish bard must surely be rewarded in heaven for every moment's pleasure given by his book.

At last it grew light. My nerves were steady now. I looked in the mirror and saw my face looking pale and wan, with signs of a wretched sleepless night. My eyes, though, shone proud and hard, despite the dark rings round them. I was satisfied with myself.

I ordered the horses to be saddled, then got dressed and went quickly down to the baths. I immersed myself in the cold Narzan water and felt my physical and mental strength return.

I came out of the bath feeling fresh and cheerful, I might have been preparing for a ball. Now try telling me that the soul doesn't depend on the body!

When I got back I found Werner in my rooms. He wore grey breeches, a short topcoat and a Circassian cap. I burst out laughing at the sight of his tiny frame beneath this enormous shaggy cap. There was nothing aggressive about his face at the best of times and on this occasion it looked even longer than usual.

'Why so sad, Doctor?' I asked. 'You've seen scores of people into the next world without turning a hair, haven't you? Pretend I've got a bilious fever. I might recover, or I might just as easily die. Try to think of me as a patient with a disease you've never met before, and you'll find it most absorbing. Now's your chance to make some interesting physiological observations on me. Don't you think the expectation of death is really a kind of malady?'

He was interested in this idea and cheered up.

We mounted and set off, with Werner clinging to the reins with both hands. In no time we had galloped past the fort, through the suburb and into the gorge along which the road twisted. The road was half overgrown with tall grass and continually crossed by a rushing stream, which had to be forded – much to the doctor's dismay, since each time his horse stopped in the water.

I can't remember a bluer, fresher morning. The sun was just peeping over the green mountain-tops, and its first warmth, mingling with the dying cool of the night, filled me with a delicious sense of ease. The joyful rays of the new day had not yet reached into the gorge and gilded only the topmost crags that overhung us on either side. The least puff of wind showered us with silver rain from the thick leafy bushes growing in the deep folds of the cliffs. I loved nature then, I remember, more than ever before. With what fascination I studied each trembling dewdrop on the broad vine leaves that reflected a million multicoloured rays. How eagerly my eyes tried to see into the hazy distance, where the road grew ever narrower and the cliffs bluer and more fearsome, till at last they appeared to join in one impenetrable wall.

We rode in silence.

'Have you made your will?' asked Werner suddenly.

'No, I've not.'

'What if you're killed?'

'The heirs will show up all right.'

'Have you no friends you'd like to send a last farewell?' he asked.

I shook my head.

'No woman even you'd like to leave a keepsake for?'

'Do you want me to open my heart to you, Doctor?' I said. 'I'm past the age when a man dies with his sweetheart's name on his lips and leaves his best friend a lock of hair (pomaded or otherwise). When I think of possible, imminent death, I think only of myself. Some people don't even do that. To hell with the friends who'll forget me in a day or, worse, tell a lot of fantastic lies about me, and the women who'll lie in another man's arms and make fun of me to stop him being jealous of the dear departed. The turmoil of life has left me with a few ideas, but no feelings. For a long time now I've lived by intellect, not feeling. I weigh and analyse my emotions and actions with strict attention, but complete detachment. There are two men within me – one lives in the full sense of the word, the other reflects and judges him. In an hour's time the first may be leaving you and the world for ever, and the second . . . who knows?

'Look, Doctor, there on the right. Do you see those three figures on the cliff? That'll be our opponents, I think.'

We spurred our horses to a trot.

Three horses were tethered in the bushes at the foot of the cliff. We tethered ours by them and made our way up a narrow path to the ledge where Grushnitsky was waiting for us with the dragoon captain and his other second, who was called Ivan Ignatievich – I never heard his surname.

The dragoon captain smiled sarcastically.

'We've been waiting for you a long time,' he said.

I took out my watch and showed it to him. He apologized and said his watch must be fast.

For a while there was an awkward silence, broken finally by Werner, who said to Grushnitsky:

'Now that you've both shown you're ready to fight and

honour's satisfied, I think you might come to terms and end the affair amicably.'

'I'm willing,' I said.

The captain winked at Grushnitsky and Grushnitsky, imagining that I was backing out, put on a very haughty look, though till then he'd been looking very pale. For the first time since our arrival he looked at me, and I saw his face was troubled and showed signs of inner conflict.

'State your conditions,' he said. 'You can be sure I shall do all I can . . .'

'My conditions are these: you make an immediate public withdrawal of your slander and apologize to me.'

'I don't know how you dare to suggest such things, sir.'

'What else could I suggest?'

'Then we'll fight.'

I shrugged my shoulders.

'Just as you like. But remember – one of us will certainly be killed.'

'I hope it's you,' he said.

'I'm sure it won't be.'

Grushnitsky blushed in confusion and gave a forced laugh.

The captain took him by the arm and led him aside. They whispered together for a long time. I had arrived in a fairly pacific frame of mind, but I was beginning to be infuriated by all this. Werner came up to me, plainly disturbed.

'Look,' he said. 'You seem to have forgotten all about their plot. I don't know how to load a pistol, but as things are. . . . You're a strange man. If you tell them you know what they're up to, they'll never dare. . . . What's the point of being shot down like a bird?'

'Please don't worry, Doctor,' I said. 'Just wait. I'll see they have no unfair advantage. Let them whisper.'

Then I said in a loud voice:

'Gentlemen, we're getting tired of waiting. If we're going to fight, then let's get on with it. You had time enough to talk yesterday.'

'We're ready,' said the captain. 'Take your places, gentlemen. Doctor, will you kindly measure out six paces?'

'Places, gentlemen,' echoed Ivan Ignatievich in a piping voice.

'Just a minute,' I said. 'I've one more condition. As we're fighting to the death we must do all we can to keep it a secret and see that our seconds aren't held responsible. Do you agree?'

'Yes, certainly.'

'Well, here's what I've thought. You see that narrow shelf up there on the right at the top of the sheer cliff? It must be a good two hundred foot drop to those sharp rocks at the bottom. If each of us stands on the edge of that shelf when the other fires, then even a slight wound will be fatal. This must accord with your wishes, since it was you who chose to fight at six paces. If one of us is wounded he'll be bound to go over and be dashed to pieces. The doctor will take out the bullet and his death can be put down to an unlucky fall. We'll draw lots to see who fires first. And let me finish by saying that I'll not fight on any other terms.'

'As you wish,' said the captain, with a meaning look at Grushnitsky, who nodded his agreement.

Grushnitsky's face was a mixture of expressions. I had put him in an awkward situation. Under normal conditions he could have aimed at my legs, given me a slight wound and had his revenge without overburdening his conscience. But now he had either to fire wide or else become a murderer – or, in the last resort, abandon his cheap trick and run the same risk as myself. I shouldn't have cared to be in his shoes at that moment.

He took the captain aside and spoke to him very heatedly. I noticed his lips were blue and trembling. But the captain turned away with a smile of contempt, and said quite loudly:

'You're a fool. You don't understand at all. Shall we go, gentlemen?'

A narrow path led through the bushes up the sheer cliff, a tottering natural stairway of broken rocks. Clinging to the bushes, we scrambled up the slope, Grushnitsky leading the way, followed by his seconds, then the doctor and me.

Werner shook me warmly by the hand.

'You're an astonishing fellow,' he said. 'Let's feel your pulse. Ha, feverish! It doesn't show in your face, though, except for a brightness in the eyes.'

There was a sudden loud rush of stones under our feet. It was Grushnitsky – he'd missed his footing when the branch he was holding broke. He would have gone sliding down on his back if his seconds hadn't supported him.

'Careful!' I shouted. 'Don't fall too soon. It's a bad omen – remember Julius Caesar.'

We had now reached the top of this jutting cliff. The ledge was covered with fine sand and might have been prepared for a duel. There were mountains all round, their peaks jostling together like an enormous flock of sheep, fading into the golden morning haze. The massive white shape of Elbrus towered in the south, closing the chain of icy peaks. Wispy clouds blowing in from the east drifted through the mountains.

I went to the edge of the shelf and looked down. My head almost reeled. Below me it was dark and cold as the grave, and jagged, moss-covered rocks, brought down by time and storms, awaited their prey.

The ledge on which we were to fight was almost a perfect triangle. Six paces were measured from the projecting corner, and it was agreed that the first to face the other's fire should stand on the edge of this corner, his back to the precipice. If he weren't killed, we should change places.

I decided to give Grushnitsky every advantage. I wanted to

test him. He might show a spark of decency after all, and then all would be well. But his weakness and vanity were bound to prevail, and I wanted to have every right to show him no mercy if fortune spared me. Who has never made such bargains with his conscience?

'Toss, Doctor,' said the captain.

Werner took a silver coin from his pocket and held it up.

'Tails!' cried Grushnitsky hastily, like a man suddenly woken by a friendly shove.

'Heads!' said I.

The coin spun up and fell with a ring to the ground. We all rushed to see it.

'You're lucky,' I said to Grushnitsky. 'You get first shot. But remember this – if you don't kill me, I promise I shan't miss.'

He flushed. He was ashamed to kill an unarmed man. I looked hard at him. For a moment I thought he was going to fall at my feet and beg my forgiveness, but how could he admit to having had such base intentions? There was only one course left to him – to fire wide, and I was sure that's what he would do. The only thing that might put him off was the thought that I would ask for a second duel.

Werner tugged my sleeve.

'Now's the time,' he said. 'You must tell them now that we know what they're about, or you're done for. Look, he's already loading. If you won't say anything, I'll tell them myself.'

'Don't do that, Doctor, whatever you do,' I said, holding him back by the arm. 'You'll spoil everything. You promised not to interfere. Why should you worry? I might want to be killed.'

He looked at me in surprise.

'Oh well,' he said, 'that's different. Only don't blame me when you're dead.'

The captain had now finished loading the pistols and gave one to Grushnitsky, smiling and whispering something as he did so, and the other to me.

I stood on the corner of the ledge, bracing my left leg firmly against a stone and leaning slightly forward to avoid toppling backwards if I got a slight wound. Grushnitsky stood opposite me and at the given signal raised his pistol. His knees were shaking, but he aimed straight at my forehead.

I seethed with fury.

Suddenly he lowered the muzzle of his pistol and turned to his second, white as a sheet.

'I can't do it,' he said in a hollow voice.

'Coward!' retorted the captain.

A shot rang out. The bullet grazed my knee, and I involuntarily took a few steps forward to get away from the edge of the cliff.

'A pity you missed, Grushnitsky, old boy,' said the captain. 'It's your turn now, so take your place. Embrace me first, though. We'll never meet again.'

They embraced, the captain scarce able to keep a straight face.

'Never fear,' he said, with a sly look at Grushnitsky. 'The world's a fool, fortune's a whore, and life's a bore.'

Having uttered this tragic statement with due solemnity, he went back to his place, and then, after a tearful embrace from Ivan Ignatievich, Grushnitsky was left facing me alone. I still can't define the feeling that surged in my breast at that moment. It was a combination of contempt, injured pride, and spite at the thought that two minutes before this man who regarded me now with such assurance and calm effrontery had, risking nothing himself, tried to kill me like a dog – for if the wound in my leg had been any worse, I'd have certainly gone over the cliff.

For a few moments I stared him hard in the face to see if there was the least sign of remorse, but I got the impression he was suppressing a smile.

'I suggest you say your prayers before dying,' I said.

'Don't worry more about my soul than you do about your own,' he answered. 'I only ask that you get on and fire your shot.'

'So you won't take back your slander? You won't apologize? Think carefully. Have you nothing on your conscience?'

'Mr Pechorin!' cried the dragoon captain. 'Let me remind you that you're not here to hold confessions. Let's get it over with. Somebody might come along the gorge and see us.'

'Very well,' I said. 'Doctor, would you come over here, please.'

He came over. Poor Werner, he was whiter than Grushnitsky had been ten minutes before.

I then spoke the following words, loudly, clearly and distinctly, the way one pronounces a death sentence.

'Doctor, these gentlemen have forgotten to put a bullet in my pistol. Through haste, I suppose. Would you mind loading it again? And make a good job of it.'

'Impossible!' cried the captain. 'Impossible! I loaded both of them. Your bullet may have rolled out, but you can't blame me for that. Anyway, you've got no right to reload, no right at all. It's quite against the rules. I won't allow it.'

'Very well,' I said. 'In that case you and I will fight on the same terms.'

That silenced him.

Grushnitsky stood with bowed head, sullen and embarrassed.

'Oh, let them be!' he finally said to the captain, who was trying to snatch my pistol from Werner. 'You know they're right.'

The captain made signs to him, but Grushnitsky wouldn't even look.

Meanwhile, the doctor loaded the pistol and handed it to me. Seeing this, the captain spat and stamped his foot.

'You're a fool,' he said, 'a downright fool. If you put me in charge, then you should do just what I say. Serves you right! Throw your life away!'

He turned and walked away, muttering 'Anyway, it's against the rules.'

'Grushnitsky,' I said, 'there's still time. Take back your slander, and I'll forgive you everything. You've not made a fool of me, so my pride is satisfied. Think, we used to be friends . . .'

His face flared.

'Shoot!' he said, his eyes flashing. 'I despise myself and hate you. If you don't kill me, I'll stab you in the back some night. The world's too small for both of us.'

I fired.

When the smoke cleared Grushnitsky was not on the ledge. There was a faint swirl of dust hanging over the edge of the cliff. Everyone cried out.

'*Finita la commedia,*' I said to Werner.

He made no reply and turned away in horror.

I shrugged my shoulders and, with a bow to Grushnitsky's seconds, I left.

As I went down the path I saw Grushnitsky's blood-stained body among the clefts in the rocks. I involuntarily closed my eyes.

I untethered my horse and set off slowly home. My heart was like lead, the sun seemed to have lost its brightness, and I felt no warmth from its rays.

Before I got to the suburb I turned right, along the valley. I was sick of the sight of humanity and wanted to be alone. I dropped the reins and rode for a long time with my head sunk on my chest and in the end found myself in a place I didn't know at all. I turned my horse back to try and find the way, but by the time I reached Kislovodsk it was past sundown. My horse and I were both fit to drop.

My servant said Werner had called and he handed me two notes, one from Werner, the other from Vera.

I opened Werner's note first. It ran as follows:

It's all gone as well as it could. The body was brought in badly disfigured and with the bullet taken out. Everyone believes he died accidentally. The commandant (who probably knew of your quarrel) shook his head, but said nothing. There's no evidence against you, so you may sleep in peace – if you can. Good-bye.

I hesitated a long time before opening the second note. What could Vera be writing to me for? I was filled with foreboding.

This is the letter. Every word is stamped indelibly on my memory.

I am writing to you in full certainty we shall never meet again. I thought the same when we parted a few years back, but heaven chose to test me once more. I failed, because my feeble heart once more obeyed the familiar voice. You won't despise me for that, will you?

This will be a farewell letter and confession in one. I must tell you all that has built up inside me since I first loved you. I shan't blame you – you treated me as any other man would have done, you loved me as a chattel, a thing to provide you with the joys, fears and sorrows without which life is dull and tedious. I realized that at the start, but you were unhappy and I sacrificed myself, hoping you'd appreciate it one day and understand how much I love you, come what may. That was a long time ago. Since then I've seen you through and through and realized my hope was vain. I was miserable, but now my love was part of me: it faded, but didn't die.

We are parting now for ever. But rest assured, I shall never love anyone else. My heart has given all it had, all its tears and hopes to you. A woman who has once loved you will always feel disdain for other men – not because you are better, no, but because there's something special in you that others haven't got, something proud and mysterious. Whatever you say, your voice has an irresistible power. No one is so persistent in his desire for love. In no one is evil so attractive. No one promises so much happiness in a look. No one knows better how to use his advantages. And no one can be so genuinely unhappy as you, because no one tries so hard to persuade himself that he isn't.

Now I must tell you why I'm leaving in such a hurry. You'll think it a trivial reason, for it only concerns me.

My husband came this morning and told me about your quarrel with Grushnitsky. My face must have shown what I felt, for he stared at me for a long time. I nearly fainted when I thought of your fighting today, and all on account of me. I thought I'd go mad, but now that I can think about it, I'm sure you won't be killed. You'll never die without me! My husband walked up and down the room for a long time. I don't know what he said, I can't remember what I answered, I probably told him that I love you. All I remember is that in the end he abused me and called me a dreadful name, and then left. I heard him order the carriage.

I've been sitting by the window for three hours now, waiting for you to come back. But I know that you're alive. You can't die without me.

The carriage is almost ready. Good-bye. I'm ruined – but what do I care? If I could be certain that you'll always remember me – not love, just remember . . .

Good-bye. There's someone coming – I must hide this letter . . .

You don't really love Mary, do you? You're not going to marry her? You must make this sacrifice for me, do you hear? I've lost everything for you.

I rushed out to the steps like a madman, leaped on my horse that was being walked round the yard, and galloped like the wind along the Pyatigorsk road. I spurred my weary horse unmercifully, and it flew along the stony road, snorting and lathered with sweat.

The sun had disappeared in a black cloud that lay on the ridge of mountains to the west, and in the valley it was dark and dank. The Podkumok threaded its way through the boulders with a dull monotonous roar.

I galloped, breathless with impatience. The thought of arriving in Pyatigorsk too late to catch Vera hammered at my heart. If only I could see her for one more minute, to say good-bye, to press her hand ... I prayed, cursed, wept, laughed. I can't describe the state of agitation and despair I was in. Now that I might lose her for ever Vera was dearer to me than anything else in the world – life, honour, happiness. God alone knows what unlikely, crazy schemes rushed through my mind.

Still I galloped on, spurring my horse without mercy, till suddenly I noticed his laboured breathing. Twice he stumbled, though the going was good. It was still three miles to Yesentuki, a Cossack village where I could get another mount, and if my horse could hold out for a few more minutes, all would be well. But, rising from a gulley at the end of the mountains, we took a sharp bend and he suddenly crashed to the ground. I sprang from the saddle and pulled the reins to try and get him up, but it was no good. He gave a faint groan through his clenched teeth and a few minutes later was dead. I was left alone in the steppe, my last hope gone. I tried walking, but my legs gave way beneath me. Worn out by the excitements of the day and my sleepless night, I fell down on the wet grass and wept like a child.

I lay there a long time, weeping bitterly, not attempting to hold back the tears and sobs. I thought my chest would burst. All my coolness and self-control vanished, my heart wilted, reason deserted me. Anyone seeing me at that moment would have turned away in contempt.

When the night dew and mountain breeze had cooled my burning head and I could think clearly again, I saw how futile and senseless it was to pursue lost happiness. What more did I want? To see her again? For what? Wasn't it all over between us? One painful farewell kiss would add nothing to my memories and would only make parting more difficult.

Still, it's nice to know I'm capable of tears! Though it may have been simply due to my being on edge, after a sleepless night and two minutes looking down the barrel of a pistol, and having an empty stomach.

It's all for the best. This new suffering has, in military jargon, 'created a successful diversion'. Crying is good for you, and if I hadn't ridden ten miles and had to walk back, I should probably have had another sleepless night. But as it was, I got back to Kislovodsk at five in the morning, threw myself on my bed and slept like Napoleon after Waterloo.

It was dark outside when I woke. I sat by the open window and undid my dressing-gown. The mountain breeze cooled my breast, which the deep sleep of fatigue had failed to calm. Lights in the distant buildings of the fort and the suburb across the river glittered through the tops of the thick limes that shaded its banks. Outside all was quiet. The princess's house was in darkness.

Werner came in. He was frowning and didn't offer his hand as he usually did. I asked him where he'd been.

'At Princess Ligovskoy's. Her daughter's ill, a nervous breakdown. That's not what I've come about, though. Look, the authorities are putting two and two together, and even if they can't prove anything definite I advise you to watch your step. The princess has just told me she knows you fought over her daughter. That old chap told her all about it – what's his name? – he saw your brush with Grushnitsky in the restaurant. I came to warn you. Good-bye. We mightn't meet again – they're liable to send you away.'

He stopped in the doorway. He wanted to shake hands, and if I'd shown the least inclination to do so, he'd have thrown his arms round me. But I remained stone cold, and he left.

People are always like that. They know all the bad sides of a thing before you do it, they help, advise, and, when they see there's no other way, they even approve of it. And then they wash their hands of it and turn away in disgust from the man who's had the guts to take on all the responsibility. They're all the same, even the best and cleverest of them.

Next morning I was ordered by the authorities to proceed to the fort at N—. I went to say good-bye to Princess Ligovskoy.

She asked if I had anything specially important to say to her and was surprised when I only said that I wished her well, etc.

'I must have a serious talk with you,' she said.

I sat down without speaking.

She obviously didn't know how to begin. She turned red in the face, her puffy fingers drummed on the table, then in the end she began in a broken voice:

'Look, Monsieur Pechorin. I believe you to be an honourable man.'

I bowed.

'In fact, I'm sure you are, though your behaviour has been rather dubious. There may be reasons for it that I don't know about, and you must tell me now what they are. You've defended my daughter's name, you fought and risked your life on her account. Don't say anything – I know you won't admit it, because Grushnitsky has been killed.' She crossed herself. 'God forgive him – and you as well, I hope. For my part, I daren't condemn you, for my daughter was the innocent cause of it all. She has told me everything – or so I think. You told her you love her, and she confessed as much to you.' She gave a deep sigh. 'But she's ill, and I'm sure this is no ordinary illness. Some secret sorrow is killing her. She won't admit it, but I'm sure that you're the cause of it.

'You may think I'm looking for rank or wealth – think

nothing of the sort. All I want is my daughter's happiness. Your present situation is an unenviable one, but it may improve. You're a man of means, my daughter loves you, and with her upbringing she'll make her husband a happy man. I am rich, and she is my only child. Tell me, what holds you back? I shouldn't be saying all this, but I trust in your heart, your honour – remember, I have but one daughter . . .'

She burst into tears.

'Princess,' I said. 'It is impossible for me to answer you. May I talk to your daughter alone?'

'Never!' she cried, rising from her chair in great agitation.

'As you wish,' I said, and made ready to go.

After a moment's thought she motioned me to wait and left the room.

Some minutes passed. My heart was pounding, but my head was cold and my mind calm. Try as I might, I couldn't find the least spark of love in me for charming Mary.

The door opened and she came in. Heavens, how she'd changed since last I saw her, such a short while before.

As she reached the middle of the room she swayed. I leaped up and helped her to an armchair.

I stood facing her. There was a long silence. Her big eyes were filled with an inexpressible sorrow and seemed to search in mine for anything akin to hope. Her pale lips made a vain effort to smile, and her delicate hands, folded in her lap, looked so thin and transparent that I pitied her.

'Princess,' I said. 'You know I was making fun of you. You must despise me.'

An unhealthy flush spread over her cheeks.

'And so,' I went on, 'you cannot love me . . .'

She turned away, rested her elbows on the table and covered her eyes. I thought I saw the glint of tears.

'My God . . .' she exclaimed, her voice barely audible.

This was getting too much for me – another minute and I'd have fallen at her feet.

'So you can see for yourself,' I said in as firm a voice as I could muster, and forcing a grin, 'It's obvious I can't marry you. Even if you wanted this now, you'd soon regret it. It's my talk with your mother that makes me speak so openly and bluntly now. I hope she's mistaken – you can easily make her think otherwise. You see me playing a mean and despicable part – I acknowledge it, but that is the most I can do for you. However badly you think of me, I accept your view. See how I debase myself – even if you loved me, you'd despise me now, wouldn't you?'

She turned to me, pale as marble, but with a glorious spark in her eyes.

'I hate you,' she said.

I thanked her, bowed politely and walked out.

An hour later I was bowling along the road from Kislovodsk in the mail. Two or three miles from Yesentuki I saw the body of my fiery steed by the roadside. The saddle was gone, probably taken by some passing Cossack, and two ravens sat in its place on the horse's back. I sighed and turned away.

Now that I'm stuck here in this fort I often look back and wonder why I didn't choose to follow the path that fate had opened to me, where there were quiet joys and peace of mind in store for me. I could never have settled to it, though. I'm like a sailor, born and bred on the deck of a privateer. Storm and battle are part of his life, and if he's cast ashore he pines in boredom, indifferent to the pleasures of shady woods and peaceful sunshine. All day long he walks the beach, listening to the steady murmur of the waves and gazing for the sight of a ship in the distant haze. He looks longingly at the pale strip between the ocean blue and the grey clouds, in hopes of seeing a sail, first like a seagull's wing, that then gradually stands out against the spray and runs in steadily towards the empty harbour.

3

THE FATALIST

ONCE I had to spend a couple of weeks in a Cossack village on the left flank. There was an infantry battalion stationed there, and each night the officers met at someone's quarters for an evening of cards.

On one occasion we sat up late at Major S—'s. We'd tired of playing boston and tossed the cards under the table. For once we had an interesting conversation – we were talking about the way many Christians accept the Muslim belief that a man's destiny is written in heaven, and everyone had some strange story to tell for or against.

'All this proves nothing, gentlemen,' said the old major. 'You quote all these odd incidents to back up your views, but none of you actually saw them happen.'

'Of course not,' said many, 'but we heard them from reliable witnesses.'

'Rubbish!' said someone. 'Where are the reliable witnesses who have seen the list with the hour of our death on it? If predestination really exists, why have we been given free-will and reason? Why do we have to give an account of our deeds?'

At this point an officer who was sitting in the corner got up and walked slowly to the table. He surveyed us with a look of calm dignity.

Lieutenant Vulich was a Serb by origin, as you could tell from his name, and his looks matched his character perfectly. He was tall, dark-complexioned, with black hair and black, piercing eyes; he had the large, though straight nose common to his race, and a cold, sad smile played perpetually on his lips. All

175

this combined to make him seem like someone apart, unable to share his thoughts and feelings with those into whose company he was thrown.

He was brave and reticent, though he had a sharp tongue. He never spoke to anyone about his personal or domestic life; he drank scarcely at all, and never ran after the Cossack girls – whose charms have to be seen to be believed. There was talk that the colonel's wife was not indifferent to his soulful eyes, but he always got extremely angry if anyone mentioned it.

There was only one passion he didn't conceal, and that was his passion for gambling. At the card table he was oblivious of everything. He usually lost, but his constant lack of success only made him more persistent. It was said that one night on picket he was keeping the bank on his pillow and having a terrific run of luck. Suddenly there were shots, the alarm was sounded and everyone jumped up and rushed for their weapons. But Vulich didn't move.

'Stake the bank,' he called to one of the most ardent punters.

'I've got a seven,' replied the punter, hurrying away.

Oblivious of the general confusion, Vulich finished the deal, and a seven came up. When he reached the firing line shots were flying thick and fast, but Vulich didn't bother about the bullets and swords of the Circassians and sought out the lucky punter. He finally spotted him among the riflemen, who were beginning to force the enemy out of the wood.

'The seven turned up,' he called, then went up to him, took out his purse and wallet and presented them to the winner, ignoring his objections about the inopportuneness of the moment. With this disagreeable task out of the way, Vulich had charged forward at the head of some soldiers and kept up a cool fire against the Circassians till the engagement ended.

We all stopped speaking when Vulich went up to the table, for everyone imagined he'd do or say something unusual.

'Gentlemen,' he said, his voice calm, though lower than usual. 'Gentlemen, what's the point of this futile arguing? You want to know if a man disposes of his own life or if his last hour is preordained. I suggest we try it out on ourselves. Who's game?'

There were shouts of 'Not me!' 'What a crazy idea!'

'What about a bet?' I asked, jokingly.

'What on?' said Vulich.

'I say there's no such thing as predestination,' I said, tipping some twenty gold pieces on to the table, all that I had in my pocket.

'Taken!' said Vulich in a hollow voice. 'Major, would you be referee? Here are fifteen gold pieces. Would you mind adding the five you owe me?'

'Very well,' said the major. 'But I really don't see what it's all about or how you're going to settle it.'

Without a word Vulich went into the major's bedroom. We followed him. He went up to a wall with weapons on it and took down at random one of the pistols of different calibres hanging there. We still couldn't see what he had in mind, but when he cocked the pistol and primed the pan, there were several who cried out and caught him by the arms.

'What are you trying to do? You're mad!' they shouted.

He freed his arms and said slowly:

'Gentlemen, which of you will pay my twenty gold pieces?'

They all walked away in silence.

Vulich went back into the other room and sat at the table. We followed and he motioned us to sit down round him. We silently obeyed. He had acquired some mysterious power over us. I looked him hard in the eyes, but he met my searching gaze with a look of steady calm and a smile flickered on his pale lips. Yet, for all his composure, I fancied I saw the mark of death on his pale face. I've noticed it myself, and I've heard a lot of old soldiers say the same, that a strange mark of inevitable doom can often be seen on the face of a man a few hours before he dies. Anyone with an eye for it is rarely mistaken.

'You're going to die today,' I said.

He turned sharply towards me, but answered slowly and calmly:

'I might, I might not.'

Then he turned to the major and asked if the pistol was loaded, but the major was so perplexed that he couldn't rightly remember.

'Come off it, Vulich!' cried someone. 'It was hanging by the bed, so it's bound to be loaded. What's the point of joking?'

'It's just a silly joke,' said someone else.

'Fifty roubles to five the pistol's not loaded!' cried another. Fresh bets were laid.

I'd had enough of all this.

'Look,' I said. 'Either shoot yourself or else put the pistol back and we'll go to bed.'

Many of the others agreed.

'Good idea. Let's go to bed,' they said.

'Gentlemen, please don't move,' said Vulich, putting the muzzle to his forehead. Everyone froze. Then he said:

'Pechorin, take a card and toss it up.'

I picked up a card from the table, I think it was the ace of hearts, and tossed it in the air. Everyone held their breath. With mingled fear and some indescribable curiosity, all eyes darted to and fro between the pistol and the fateful ace. It fluttered in the air and floated slowly down. As it touched the table, Vulich pulled the trigger. The pistol misfired.

There were cries of 'Thank God! It wasn't loaded.'

'Let's just see, though,' said Vulich, cocking it again and aiming at a cap hanging over the window. A shot rang out and the room filled with smoke. When it had cleared, the cap was taken down – there was a hole straight through the middle and the bullet was embedded in the wall.

For two or three minutes everyone was speechless, while Vulich calmly put my gold pieces in his purse. Then everyone started to explain why the pistol hadn't gone off the first time. Some said the pan had been dirty, others suggested in undertones that the powder was damp the first time and that Vulich had then added some fresh powder. But I said that this wasn't true, for I'd not once taken my eyes off the pistol the whole time.

'You've got gambler's luck,' I said to Vulich.

'For once in my life,' he said, smiling with satisfaction. 'This is better than faro or banker.'

'Rather more dangerous, though.'

'Well, do you believe in predestination now?' he asked.

'Yes, I believe in it,' I said, 'but I can't understand why I was so sure you were going to die today.'

And this man who, just before, had been calmly pointing a pistol at his own forehead now suddenly got upset and annoyed.

'That'll do!' he said, getting up. 'Our bet's over now and you've no business saying things like that.'

He picked up his cap and left. It struck me as odd – and not without reason.

Soon everyone went home, each offering his own explanation of Vulich's eccentricities, and probably all agreeing that I'd been selfish to bet against a man who was going to shoot himself – as though he needed me to provide an opportunity!

I walked home through the empty back streets of the village. A full red moon was just showing over the broken line of buildings, like the glare of a fire. Stars shone calmly in the deep blue sky, and I was amused to think that there were once wise men who imagined the stars took part in men's petty squabbles over a patch of land or somebody's 'rights'. While in fact these lamps, which they supposed had been lit for the sole purpose of shining on their battles and triumphs, still burn on as bright as ever, while they, with all their passions and hopes, have long since vanished, like a fire lit by some carefree traveller at the edge of a forest. Yet what strength they derived from this certainty that the heavens with all their countless hosts looked down on them in silent, but never-failing sympathy. And we, their pitiful descendants, drift through the world, without beliefs, pride, pleasure or fear, except that automatic fear that grips us when we think of the certainty of death. We can no longer make great sacrifices for the good of mankind, or even for our own happiness, because we know they are unattainable. And as our ancestors rushed from illusion to illusion, so we drift indifferently from doubt to doubt. But, unlike them, we have no hope, nor even that indefinable but real sense of pleasure that's felt in any struggle, be it with men or destiny.

Many similar thoughts ran through my mind, but I didn't dwell on them, for I'm not given to brooding on abstract ideas. It gets you nowhere. As a boy I was a dreamer and dwelt with loving care on the dark and radiant images traced by my rest-less, eager fancy. And what did it bring me? Weariness, as though I'd spent a night wrestling a phantom, and a vague, regretful memory. In this fruitless struggle I wasted all the ardour and drive that are needed in real life, and when I came to life itself, I had been through everything mentally before and found it boring and disgusting, like reading a poor pastiche of a long familiar book.

The events of the evening had made a considerable impres-sion on me and set me on edge. I'm not sure now if I believe in predestination or not, but that evening I had no doubts of it at all. We'd had striking proof of it, and though I'd ridiculed

our ancestors and their obliging astrology, I now found myself
taking the same line. However, I stopped myself from going
too far along this perilous path, and since I make it a rule never
to reject or believe in anything absolutely, I turned from metaphysical speculations to attend to the ground under my feet.
This proved a very timely precaution, for I tripped and almost
fell over something plump and soft, though not, apparently,
alive. The moon was shining straight on to the road, and I bent
down to see what it was. Before me lay a pig sliced in half by a
sword.

I'd barely had time to inspect it when I heard steps and saw
two Cossacks come running out of a side-street. One of them
came up and asked if I'd seen a drunken Cossack chasing a pig.
I told them I'd seen no Cossack, but pointed to the unlucky
victim of his reckless daring.

'The scoundrel!' said the second Cossack. 'He gets a skinful
of *chikhir* and then goes off on the rampage. Come on, Yere-
meich, we'd better go after him and get him tied up, or he
might . . .'

They went off, and I walked on, taking extra care, till I was
safely home.

I was lodging with an old Cossack sergeant, a man I liked for
his kindly nature and – more particularly – for his pretty
daughter Nastya. She was waiting for me by the gate as usual,
wrapped in a fur coat. It was a chilly night and in the moonlight
I saw her sweet lips were blue with cold. She smiled when she
saw me, but I was in no mood to stop and merely said good-
night to her and walked past. She was going to reply, but only
sighed.

I shut my door behind me, lit the candle and threw myself
down on the bed. I was longer than usual going to sleep and
there was a pale light in the eastern sky by the time I did get off.
That night, however, I was *not* predestined to sleep undisturbed.

At four in the morning a pair of fists pounded at my window. I leaped up to see what it was. There were shouts of 'Get up and get dressed.' I scrambled into my clothes and went outside.

Three officers had come for me. They were white as a sheet and all spoke at once.

'Do you know what's happened?'

'No,' I said. 'What?'

'Vulich has been killed.'

I was stunned.

'Yes, killed,' they said. 'Come on, quick!'

'Where are we going?'

'We'll tell you on the way.'

We set off, and they told me what had happened, interspersing their story with comments on the strange quirk of fate that had saved Vulich from certain death only half an hour before he had died. He'd been walking alone down the dark street when along came the drunken Cossack who had killed the pig. The fellow might have gone by without seeing him, if Vulich hadn't suddenly stopped and asked him who he was looking for. 'You!' said the Cossack, and struck him a blow with his sword that split him from the shoulder almost down to the heart. The two Cossacks I'd seen chasing the murderer had come along and picked up the wounded man, but he was on the point of death and said only three words: 'He was right'. I alone realized what these mysterious words meant – they referred to me, for I had unthinkingly foretold the poor fellow's death. My instinct hadn't failed me – I had in fact seen the mark of death in the changed look on his face.

We were making our way to an empty cottage at the end of the village where the murderer had locked himself in. Droves of wailing women were heading the same way, and an occasional Cossack dashed belatedly into the street, hastily buckling on his dagger and running on ahead of us. There was terrible confusion.

At last we arrived at the cottage. The doors and shutters were fastened from the inside. A crowd stood round, officers and Cossacks held heated discussions, women wailed and lamented. I was immediately struck by the expressive face of an old woman in the crowd who was looking frantic with despair. She sat on a thick log, her elbows on her knees, holding her head in her hands. It was the murderer's mother. Now and then her lips moved – it might have been a whispered prayer, or a curse.

Meanwhile we had to decide on some way of seizing him, but nobody was anxious to be the first in. I went up to the window and looked through the crack of the shutter. He lay on the floor, a pistol in his right hand, a blood-stained sword by his side. He was pale, his expressive eyes rolled furiously, and every now and then he shuddered and clasped his head, as though hazily recalling the events of the night. There seemed so little resolution in his troubled look that I told the major it would be better for the Cossacks to break down the door and go in now, rather than wait till he had come fully to his senses.

Just then an old Cossack captain went up to the door and called the murderer's name. He answered.

'You've done wrong, Yefimich,' said the captain. 'All you can do now is give yourself up.'

'I won't!' said the Cossack.

'Have a conscience, man. You're an honest Christian, aren't you, not some plaguey Chechen? If you do wrong, you must just face up to it and take what comes.'

'I won't do it!' cried the Cossack menacingly, and we heard the click of a pistol being cocked.

The captain spoke to the old woman.

'Here, Mother,' he said. 'Have a word with your boy. He might listen to you. He's only making it worse for himself with the Almighty, carrying on like this. And besides, he's been keeping these gentlemen standing about for two hours.'

The old woman stared at him and shook her head.

He went up to the major.

'He won't give himself up, sir,' he said. 'I know him. If we break in, he'll do for a good many of our lads. Would you like us to shoot him? The crack in the shutter's wide enough.'

Just then I had an odd idea. Like Vulich, I decided to put fate to the test.

'Half a minute,' I said to the major. 'I'll get him alive.'

I told the captain to engage him in conversation and posted three Cossacks by the door ready to smash it in and come to my aid when I gave the signal. Then I went round the cottage to the fatal window. My heart was pounding.

The captain called to the Cossack:

'Damn you! Having us on, are you? Or do you think we won't get you?'

Then he started banging at the door with all his might. Through the crack in the shutter I watched the movements of the Cossack, who was not expecting an attack from this quarter, then suddenly I tore off the shutter and threw myself head first through the window. There was a shot just by my ear and the bullet ripped an epaulette from my shoulder. The room filled with smoke and my adversary couldn't find the sword that lay beside him. I grabbed his arms, the Cossacks burst in, and within three minutes the criminal had been bound and taken away under escort. The crowd dispersed, and the officers congratulated me – as well they might!

How can one not be a fatalist after this? Yet who really knows if he believes a thing or not? How often our beliefs are mere illusions or mental aberrations.

I prefer to doubt everything. Such an attitude makes no difference to a man's determination – on the contrary, as far as I am concerned, I always go more boldly forward when I don't know what lies ahead. After all, the worst you can do is die, and you've got to die some time.

On the way back to the fort I told Maxim Maximych about all that I'd seen and experienced, and asked him what he thought about predestination. At first he didn't understand the word, but I explained it as best I could, whereupon he shook his head meaningly and said:

'Well, yes, of course. . . . It's a tricky problem. As a matter of fact, those Asian triggers often don't work if they're not well oiled, or if you don't press hard enough. I don't go much on Circassian rifles either. Don't seem right for us somehow, and you're like as not to get your nose burnt with that short butt they've got. Their swords, though, now they really are something.'

He thought a bit, then added:

'Bad luck on that poor chap, though. He should have known better than talk to drunks after dark. Still, I suppose that's how he was meant to die . . .'

That's all I could get out of him – he's not at all keen on metaphysical discussions.

THE END

FOR THE BEST IN PAPERBACKS, LOOK FOR THE 🐧

In every corner of the world, on every subject under the sun, Penguin represents quality and variety – the very best in publishing today.

For complete information about books available from Penguin – including Puffins, Penguin Classics and Arkana – and how to order them, write to us at the appropriate address below. Please note that for copyright reasons the selection of books varies from country to country.

In the United Kingdom: Please write to *Dept E.P., Penguin Books Ltd, Harmondsworth, Middlesex, UB7 0DA.*

If you have any difficulty in obtaining a title, please send your order with the correct money, plus ten per cent for postage and packaging, to *PO Box No 11, West Drayton, Middlesex*

In the United States: Please write to *Dept BA, Penguin, 299 Murray Hill Parkway, East Rutherford, New Jersey 07073*

In Canada: Please write to *Penguin Books Canada Ltd, 2801 John Street, Markham, Ontario L3R 1B4*

In Australia: Please write to the *Marketing Department, Penguin Books Australia Ltd, P.O. Box 257, Ringwood, Victoria 3134*

In New Zealand: Please write to the *Marketing Department, Penguin Books (NZ) Ltd, Private Bag, Takapuna, Auckland 9*

In India: Please write to *Penguin Overseas Ltd, 706 Eros Apartments, 56 Nehru Place, New Delhi, 110019*

In the Netherlands: Please write to *Penguin Books Netherlands B.V., Postbus 195, NL–1380AD Weesp*

In West Germany: Please write to *Penguin Books Ltd, Friedrichstrasse 10–12, D–6000 Frankfurt Main 1*

In Spain: Please write to *Longman Penguin España, Calle San Nicolas 15, E–28013 Madrid*

In Italy: Please write to *Penguin Italia s.r.l., Via Como 4, I-20096 Pioltello (Milano)*

In France: Please write to *Penguin Books Ltd, 39 Rue de Montmorency, F-75003 Paris*

In Japan: Please write to *Longman Penguin Japan Co Ltd, Yamaguchi Building, 2–12–9 Kanda Jimbocho, Chiyoda-Ku, Tokyo 101*

FOR THE BEST IN PAPERBACKS, LOOK FOR THE 🐧

PENGUIN CLASSICS

Netochka Nezvanova Fyodor Dostoyevsky

Dostoyevsky's first book tells the story of 'Nameless Nobody' and introduces many of the themes and issues which will dominate his great masterpieces.

Selections from the Carmina Burana A verse translation by David Parlett

The famous songs from the *Carmina Burana* (made into an oratorio by Carl Orff) tell of lecherous monks and corrupt clerics, drinkers and gamblers, and the fleeting pleasures of youth.

Fear and Trembling Søren Kierkegaard

A profound meditation on the nature of faith and submission to God's will which examines with startling originality the story of Abraham and Isaac.

Selected Prose Charles Lamb

Lamb's famous essays (under the strange pseudonym of Elia) on anything and everything have long been celebrated for their apparently innocent charm; this major new edition allows readers to discover the darker and more interesting aspects of Lamb.

The Picture of Dorian Gray Oscar Wilde

Wilde's superb and macabre novella, one of his supreme works, is reprinted here with a masterly Introduction and valuable Notes by Peter Ackroyd.

A Treatise of Human Nature David Hume

A universally acknowledged masterpiece by 'the greatest of all British Philosophers' – A. J. Ayer

FOR THE BEST IN PAPERBACKS, LOOK FOR THE 🐧

PENGUIN CLASSICS

A Passage to India   E. M. Forster

Centred on the unresolved mystery in the Marabar Caves, Forster's great work provides the definitive evocation of the British Raj.

The Republic   Plato

The best-known of Plato's dialogues, *The Republic* is also one of the supreme masterpieces of Western philosophy whose influence cannot be overestimated.

The Life of Johnson   James Boswell

Perhaps the finest 'life' ever written, Boswell's *Johnson* captures for all time one of the most colourful and talented figures in English literary history.

Remembrance of Things Past (3 volumes)   Marcel Proust

This revised version by Terence Kilmartin of C. K. Scott Moncrieff's original translation has been universally acclaimed – available for the first time in paperback.

Metamorphoses   Ovid

A golden treasury of myths and legends which has proved a major influence on Western literature.

A Nietzsche Reader   Friedrich Nietzsche

A superb selection from all the major works of one of the greatest thinkers and writers in world literature, translated into clear, modern English.

FOR THE BEST IN PAPERBACKS, LOOK FOR THE

PENGUIN CLASSICS

Anton Chekhov	**The Duel and Other Stories**
	The Kiss and Other Stories
	Lady with Lapdog and Other Stories
	Plays (The Cherry Orchard/Ivanov/The Seagull/Uncle Vanya/The Bear/The Proposal/A Jubilee/Three Sisters
	The Party and Other Stories
Fyodor Dostoyevsky	**The Brothers Karamazov**
	Crime and Punishment
	The Devils
	The Gambler/Bobok/A Nasty Story
	The House of the Dead
	The Idiot
	Netochka Nezvanova
	Notes From Underground and **The Double**
Nikolai Gogol	**Dead Souls**
	Diary of a Madman and Other Stories
Maxim Gorky	**My Apprenticeship**
	My Childhood
	My Universities
Mikhail Lermontov	**A Hero of Our Time**
Alexander Pushkin	**Eugene Onegin**
	The Queen of Spades and Other Stories
Leo Tolstoy	**Anna Karenin**
	Childhood/Boyhood/Youth
	The Cossacks/The Death of Ivan Ilyich/Happy Ever After
	The Kreutzer Sonata and Other Stories
	Master and Man and Other Stories
	Resurrection
	The Sebastopol Sketches
	War and Peace
Ivan Turgenev	**Fathers and Sons**
	First Love
	Home of the Gentry
	A Month in the Country
	On the Eve
	Rudin
	Sketches from a Hunter's Album
	Spring Torrents